She placed her elbows on the table and leaned forward, her gaze so intent Bo felt as if she were somehow peering inside his soul.

"So, are you in for a little crime investigation?"

The fresh, slightly floral scent of her perfume drifted across the table as her gaze continued to hold him captive. He had arrived at the high school not knowing what his decision was, whether he intended to try to find the real killer or get out of this town as fast as possible.

The light of her belief in him shone from her eyes. He bathed in it and realized he wanted this...his innocence restored among the people who had once been friends and neighbors.

"I'm in," he finally said. He hoped in making that decision he hadn't just made a mistake he would come to regret. Asking questions, talking to people and stirring up everything from the past also might stir up a killer's rage.

SCENE OF THE CRIME: KILLER COVE

New York Times Bestselling Author
CARLA CASSIDY

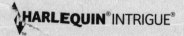

Recycling programs
for this product may
not exist in your area.

ISBN-13: 978-0-373-69832-5

Scene of the Crime: Killer Cove

Copyright © 2015 by Carla Bracale

Printed in U.S.A.

www.Harlequin.com

Carla Cassidy is a *New York Times* bestselling author who has written more than one hundred books for Harlequin. Carla believes the only thing better than curling up with a good book to read is sitting down at the computer with a good story to write. She's looking forward to writing many more books and bringing hours of pleasure to readers.

Books by Carla Cassidy

HARLEQUIN INTRIGUE

Visit the Author Profile page at Harlequin.com for more titles.

CAST OF CHARACTERS

Bo McBride—Accused but not charged with the murder of his girlfriend, Shelly Sinclair, two years before. Bo had left his hometown, but now is back and looking for justice.

Claire Silver—A schoolteacher and one of the few people in town who believes Bo is innocent. Claire also has a secret admirer who turns into a dangerous stalker as she and Bo grow closer.

Jimmy Tambor—Bo's best friend, but is he really happy to see his old friend back in town?

Coach Roger Cantor—Has his friendship with Claire transformed into something dark and dangerous?

Eric Baptiste—Grew up in the swamp next to Claire. Has his friendship turned to romantic obsession?

Neil Sampson—City councilman whom Claire dated briefly. Does this spurned lover have a score to settle with her?

Mac Sinclair—Shelly's older brother. He believes Bo killed his sister. Does he see harming Claire as a perverted form of justice?

Chapter One

Bo McBride throttled down, the Harley responding by slowing as he passed the old, faded wooden sign that read Lost Lagoon, Population 705.

His stomach knotted painfully as the scent of the swamp not only surrounded him but invaded his lungs, making it difficult to breathe around the anxiety and anger the scent of home now brought.

As far as almost everyone in town was concerned, it had been two years since he'd been back to Lost Lagoon, Mississippi. Only two people knew about his monthly visits back here to his mother's place, secret visits that had him arriving and leaving under the cover of darkness.

He wouldn't be here now if his mother hadn't passed away unexpectedly two days before. A massive heart attack. His best friend, Jimmy Tambor, who had moved into the house when Bo left town, had given him the grim news.

It had taken Bo an entire day to process the fact that his mother was gone and another day to make arrangements with his employees to leave. The funeral was to be held tomorrow. After that, he figured it would take a couple of days to put his mother's things in order and then get the hell away from the town that had robbed him of the last two years of his mother's life, among other things.

He'd been on the road for hours, leaving his place in Jackson before dawn that morning. He hadn't stopped to eat except snacks picked up at gas station pit stops, and now decided before showing up at his childhood home that he'd grab a quick bite to eat at George's Diner, located just inside the city limits.

George's Diner was more glorified hamburger joint than true diner. Although there were a couple of booths inside, most people either drove through or sat at the wooden counter to be served as quickly as possible.

Bo parked his ride on the side of the building and then pulled off his helmet and hand-combed his thick, shaggy hair. He stretched and headed around the building to the front door, eager to escape the June heat and humidity.

It was after three and few people were inside. The prevalent scent was of fried onions, hot grease and the gamy odor of swamp fish and gator. There was a pretty blonde woman serving a couple at one of the tables.

Bo slid onto the first stool at the counter just as George stepped out of the kitchen. George King was a big man, both tall and weighing in at about three hundred pounds of muscle and fat. He was bald, with thick black eyebrows and dark brown eyes that narrowed the instant he saw Bo. He ambled over to Bo as he wiped his hands on his stained white apron.

"Burger, fries and a sweet tea," Bo said.

"Move along, Bo. I don't serve murderers here," George replied, his deep voice filled with disgust.

His words aroused Bo's anger—the anger of injustice, of things unchanged and memories of the isolation and despair he'd felt when he'd left town two years before.

He wanted to fight for the simple dignity of being served a burger, but instead he slid off the stool and left the building without saying a word.

He certainly hadn't expected to be welcomed back to town with open arms, but he also hadn't expected the same kind of intense animosity that had ultimately forced him to leave.

Sitting on his bike, he tried to school his emotions. Jimmy was meeting him at the house and he didn't want to carry any more anger with him than what already burned in his soul. It had just been a hamburger and fries, after all, and everyone in town knew that George was an ass.

He pulled on his helmet and was just about to start his motorcycle when he heard somebody call out his name. From around the corner of the diner the curly-haired blonde waitress appeared. He had a quick impression of long, shapely legs, big blue eyes and a warm smile that was as surprising as a gator wearing a straw hat.

She tossed him a brown paper bag that he caught with his hands. "Burger and fries. I couldn't do anything about the sweet tea," she said, and then before he could reply she disappeared back around the corner of the building.

Bo sat in stunned surprise for several moments. It had been an unexpected gesture of kindness. He opened the bag and ate the food. At the same time he wondered who the woman was and why she had gone to the trouble.

It was almost four o'clock when he drove slowly down the street that was an outer band. Several blocks over to his left was the business area of Lost Lagoon, and on his right was the swamp side of town with a few small, neat cabins intermixed among weather-faded, neglected shanties. The swamp was an overgrown, tangled bog about twenty feet from the back of these houses and continued until Bo made the left curve that would skirt the edges of the lagoon.

On the right side of the lagoon, the swamp ended and he was on higher ground with larger homes and an aura of better prosperity. He made two turns to take him into the neighborhood where he'd grown up.

It appeared as if nothing had changed in the time he'd been gone. Only when he noticed a lot of new construction at the top of a hill behind his neighborhood did he realize something was about to change in the tiny town.

At the sight of the neat white ranch house with black shutters and a butterfly wind chime hanging off the edge of the small porch, his heart fluttered with grief. He pulled into the driveway and parked and wished that the past two years had been different.

He didn't bother taking anything from his saddlebags. He had plenty of time to unpack what few things he'd brought with him. He climbed off the bike, set his helmet on the seat and then headed for the front door.

As he stepped up on the porch the door swung open and Jimmy Tambor pulled him into a bro hug. "I'm sorry, Bo. I'm so damned sorry," he said and released Bo.

"Thanks," Bo said woodenly.

"If it's any consolation at all, the doctor thinks it happened in her sleep," Jimmy replied. "She just went to bed as usual and I found her in the morning. I don't think she suffered."

Bo hoped that was the case. His mother had suffered enough five years ago when his father had passed away in a car accident. At that time Bo had feared his mother would grieve herself to death.

Jimmy had moved into the house when Bo had left town. Bo had wanted somebody he trusted to be there for his mother while he couldn't be.

"I don't know how to thank you for everything you've done for me and for her since I left town," Bo finally said.

"You know she was like a mother to me, too," Jimmy replied, his brown eyes a perfect match for the thatch of unruly hair on his head. "Come on, let's get out of the heat. I've got a couple of cold beers in the fridge with our names on them."

Bo stepped into the house behind Jimmy, and the first thing he noticed was the lack of scent. Even on the day Bo had left town the house had smelled of freshly baked chocolate chip cookies.

His mother had loved to cook and bake, and never had Bo been in the house when the fragrance of her labors hadn't filled the air. It was then that his true grief began.

The pain stabbed him through his heart, leaving him momentarily breathless. He'd felt pain this deep only once before in his life and that had been on the night two years ago that Shelly Sinclair had been found murdered, her body floating in the lagoon.

He sucked it up and stuffed it down, knowing the time to truly grieve would come later, when he was all alone. He followed Jimmy through the spotlessly clean living room and into the kitchen. Jimmy pulled two bottles of beer from the refrigerator and Bo sat at the round wooden table where he'd spent most of his life eating meals with his mother and father.

When his father died, Bo had moved from his apartment on the third floor of his business and back into the house with his mother. He hadn't wanted her alone with her grief, and the return to his childhood home had gone seamlessly.

Jimmy set one bottle of beer in front of Bo and then sat with his own bottle across from his friend. They unscrewed lids and each took a drink. Jimmy set his bottle on the table and leaned back in his chair.

"There will be a simple graveside service tomorrow at three," he said. "Your mother had all the arrangements already made. When I moved in here she told me where to find her important paperwork and that she'd left a will with Grey Davis. I'm sure he'll want you to get in touch with him."

Bo waved a hand and took another drink of his beer. "I'll get in touch with him sometime after tomorrow's service."

"How long are you planning on staying?"

"As briefly as possible," Bo replied. "I stopped by George's place to get a burger on the way in. He refused to serve me." He tried to keep the bitterness out of his voice.

"You want a sandwich? I've got some ham and cheese." Jimmy started to rise from his chair but Bo waved him back down.

"Actually, I was getting ready to pull away from George's and some pretty blonde woman ran out with a burger and fries for me." Bo thought of the warmth of her smile and figured she must be new to town and didn't know that he was the prime suspect in his girlfriend's murder.

"Curly hair?" Jimmy asked.

"And long legs," Bo replied.

"That would be Claire Silver."

"Is she new in town?"

Jimmy shook his head. "No, she's been here all her life. She's three or four years younger than us, so you probably just never noticed her."

Bo took another sip of his beer, mentally acknowledging Jimmy's words. From the time he was seventeen, he hadn't noticed any other girl except Shelly Sinclair. Shelly had been his high school crush, then his girlfriend, then his lover and finally a murder victim.

"I'm assuming things are going well at the bar," Bo said, needing to get thoughts of the past out of his head.

"Business is booming, but you should know that by the profits we're turning. In fact, I should probably get out of here pretty quickly because the dinner rush usually starts soon. I just wanted to be here when you arrived. I didn't want you walking into an empty house."

"I appreciate that," Bo replied.

"I've still got all my things in the guest bedroom. I plan to rent an apartment, but haven't had a chance to get it done yet. If you could give me a couple of days..." Jimmy let his voice trail off.

"There's no reason why you can't continue to stay here. I'll only be here maybe a week at the most. The house is paid for and at this point I don't need to sell it."

"We'll see how you feel about it later," Jimmy replied. He finished his beer and stood. "I'll be back here around three or so. I'll try to be quiet so I don't wake you."

Bo stood to walk his friend to the door. "Hope you have a good night."

Jimmy flashed him a boyish grin. "Every night is a good night at Jimmy's Place. We'll talk more sometime tomorrow." He gave Bo a clap on the shoulder and then left the house.

Bo went into the living room and slumped down on one end of the sofa. Jimmy's Place. It had actually been Bo's Place before the murder. During the late afternoons and early evenings, families had filled the dining room, drawn to the good food, the reasonable prices and the atmosphere of community and goodwill. At ten, the diners had mostly gone and the drinkers and partiers arrived.

It was only after Bo had been named as the number-one suspect in Shelly's murder that the families stopped coming in and even the staunchest alcoholic refused to frequent the place.

Within a week Bo had become a pariah in town with only his mother and Jimmy sticking by his side. There had been no evidence to warrant Bo's arrest, but in the eyes of Lost Lagoon he'd been deemed guilty and judged as such.

A month after Shelly's murder it had been his mother who had urged him to get out of town, to start fresh someplace else.

With his life and business in shambles and the woman he'd loved dead, Bo had finally left Lost Lagoon.

Although he still owned what had once been Bo's Place, as far as everyone in town knew, Jimmy had bought the place, and under the new name, business was once again booming.

Bo snagged a second beer from the refrigerator and then spent the next hour sipping his drink and wandering the house. Little had changed. The bedroom where he had stayed while he'd lived here looked as if he'd just stepped out for a meal rather than been gone for so long. The smaller guest bedroom held signs of Jimmy's takeover. The closet door hung open, displaying a variety of clothing including half a dozen black shirts with the white lettering reading Jimmy's Place on the pocket.

Finally he entered his mother's room with its attached bathroom. Apparently Jimmy had worked hard to remove all traces of the death scene. He sat on the edge of the bed and ran his hand over the patchwork quilt in shades of pink and rose, a lump the size of Mississippi in the back of his throat.

He and his mother had usually spoken on the phone at least once every couple of days. He'd talked to her days ago and while she'd sounded a bit frail and weak, she'd assured him she'd just picked up a bug of some kind and that Jimmy was feeding her chicken soup and she'd be fine.

Dammit, Bo should have been here. He should have taken her to the doctor, he should have eaten dinner with her the night of her death and every night in the last two years.

His occasional visits had been short and bittersweet. He'd arrive in the middle of the night on a Saturday, park his motorcycle in her garage so the neighbors wouldn't know he was there, and then leave again in the middle of the night on Sunday.

He'd known it would be easier on his mom if people in town didn't know he was at her home. She'd carried the stigma of being a murderer's mother although she'd never mentioned her own alienation from friends and neighbors.

Bo wasn't sure how long he sat there. He had no more tears left, having spent them on the day he'd gotten the call from Jimmy that his mother was gone.

He was vaguely surprised that it was almost seven when he finally left his mother's bedroom. He needed to get his things from the motorcycle and settle in for the night. If Jimmy continued to stay here, then all Bo needed to do was bury his mother, meet with the lawyer and pack up his mom's clothing and shoes and other items to donate.

It was Wednesday night. He figured if things went smoothly and he used his time wisely, then by Sunday he could be back on the road to return to the life he'd been forced to build, a new life he'd never wanted.

Bo McBride was back.

Nothing exciting ever happened in Lost Lagoon, not since Shelly Sinclair's murder, and that had been tragic.

Claire Silver had heard about Bo's mother's death and assumed he'd come back to take care of whatever needed to be done. His presence here was sure to stir people up.

George had certainly been stirred up. He'd seen her toss the bag of food to Bo and had fired her. Claire had gone home and spent the late afternoon cleaning house, her thoughts whirling about Bo.

She'd never believed in his guilt. Nothing she'd heard had ever changed her mind about Bo's innocence in Shelly's death. She believed he'd been a victim of an overzealous sheriff with tunnel vision that had zeroed in on Bo as the perpetrator, to the exclusion of anyone else.

She hoped he was back not just to bury his mother, but also to clear his name, because if he was innocent, as Claire believed, then a killer was walking free in the town.

At six thirty she grabbed a can of pepper spray and stuck it in her back pocket. After unlocking her bicycle from the porch, she took off riding. She rode most nights, pedaling at a leisurely pace away from her "swamp home" and to the outer band that would take her around the lagoon.

This was her time to unwind from the day, to wave to neighbors and empty her mind of any stresses, which were few in her life at the moment.

Normally when she reached the edge of the lagoon she turned to head down Main Street, but instead this evening she continued around the outer road and then on impulse turned onto the roads that would take her to Bo McBride's home.

When she reached his house she stopped and got off her bike, leaning it against the white picket fence along the boundary of the yard.

She had no idea what she was doing here. Had no indication of what her intentions might be. Did she want to officially welcome him to the town that had effectively driven him out two years ago? Did she want to extend her sympathies about his mother? She'd scarcely known his mother. She'd been a shy, retiring woman rarely seen around town.

Claire grabbed her bicycle and was about to get back on it when the front door of the house flew open and Bo walked out. His blue eyes narrowed as he slowed his steps. She leaned the bike against the fence one again.

"What are you? My new resident stalker? Are you one of those women who writes to serial murderers in prison? Buy sick memorabilia on the internet from crime scenes?" His voice was rife with distrust.

"Actually, I'm the woman who fed you this afternoon and lost my job in the process," she replied evenly. "I suppose a simple thank-you is too much to ask for."

Bo grimaced and raked a hand through his thick, unruly black hair. "Sorry, I was way out of line." He motioned her closer and frowned. "You lost your job?"

"Don't worry about it. George fires me at least once a week and besides, it's just a job to alleviate some of my boredom during the summers. My real job is teaching second graders. By the way, my name is Claire Silver."

"I'm sure you know who I am. Bo McBride, who, according to everyone in Lost Lagoon, is the man who got away with murder."

"Not everyone," Claire replied. She'd forgotten how utterly sexy Bo was with his broad shoulders and lean hips and long legs. She'd always thought him handsome and she'd always thought of him as belonging to Shelly.

He raised a dark brow at the same time he pulled a duffel from one of his saddlebags. "You think I'm innocent? That's novel. There aren't many in town who share your view."

"I've never been much of a blind follower. I prefer to think for myself and come to my own conclusions," she replied.

Bo pulled another duffel from the opposite saddlebag and dropped it to the concrete driveway. He gazed at her curiously, as if she might be an alien from another planet.

"So, how did you come to the conclusion that I'm innocent?"

A wave of unusual shyness suddenly swept through her. She didn't want to tell him all the reasons she believed he wasn't capable of killing Shelly. It would be like sharing a little piece of her soul, a portrait of a romance that would make her look strange.

"Let's just say it's a long story. I was sorry to hear about your mother," she said in an attempt to change the topic of conversation.

The stark grief that swept over his face was there only a moment and then gone, but it was enough for Claire's heart to respond. She had no memories of her own mother, and she couldn't imagine the pain over the loss of his while he'd been virtually banished from his home…from his mother.

"Thanks. It came as quite a shock." He picked

up his duffel bags. "I'm sorry about your job and I appreciate your kindness this afternoon."

"No big deal." She grabbed her bike and got on it. Darkness came early around the lagoon and on the swamp side of town, and she liked to be inside by nightfall. "I guess I'll see you around," she said and with a wave, she pedaled away from his driveway.

She wasn't sure what had driven her to go to his home and stop other than curiosity. There was no question that he was apparently wary of interacting with anyone, and why wouldn't he be?

He'd always been handsome, but the past two years had added lines to his lean face that gave it new character that only enhanced his sexiness. Not that it mattered to her. In her mind he would always be Shelly's man, part of a couple who for Claire had been a shining example of what love should look like.

She pedaled a little faster as she rounded the lagoon where the June twilight appeared darker, gloomier. As always, when her home came into view a sense of pride swelled up inside her.

Two years ago her home had looked a lot like so many of the other broken, faded shanties that lined the street. It had taken most of her first year's salary as a teacher to almost completely rebuild the one-bedroom hellhole where she'd grown up into a pretty cottage with up-to-date plumbing and newly painted walls and a sense of permanence.

For so many years it had just been a place to survive. Now it was her sanctuary, a place that held no memories of her crummy childhood.

When she reached her porch she lifted her bike up the three stairs and chained it to the railing, at the same time noticing the small vase of flowers that sat just outside her front door.

So, her "secret admirer" had struck again. This was the third time in as many weeks she'd found flowers and a note on her doorstep.

The first time the flowers had appeared with a note that simply read, *From your secret admirer.* Claire had found it a little bit charming and a little bit silly. She'd assumed that the admirer would make himself known to her as she had no idea who it might be.

The second vase of flowers had appeared with a note that indicated he was thinking about her. She thought the flowers might be from Neil Sampson, a city councilman she'd dated for about two months and had broken up with about six months before. Neil hadn't taken the breakup well, and she wondered if the little floral treats were an attempt to win her back.

She grabbed the new vase, unlocked her door and then stepped inside. She set the flowers and the folded note on the table and headed directly to the refrigerator for a cold bottle of water.

She unscrewed the lid and leaned against the nearby cabinet as she sipped the cold liquid. Thoughts of Bo instantly filled her mind. She'd heard rumors that he'd moved to Jackson and had opened a bar and grill there. Had he found love with some new woman?

Two years was a long time to mourn, and he was a healthy, vital twenty-eight-year-old male who would certainly not have any trouble gaining women's interest.

She finished the water, tossed the bottle into the recycle bin in her pantry and then walked back to the table where the vase of flowers and the note awaited her.

The vase was a small clear white glass that could be picked up most places for a dollar or so, and the flowers weren't from a floral shop but rather hand-picked.

It would be difficult to try to track down where it had come from even if she was of the mind to conduct a little investigation, and she wasn't inclined to do so. Whoever it was would eventually stop with the anonymous gestures and show himself.

She opened the note. *You look so pretty in pink*, it read. She glanced down at the pink tank top she wore and frowned, a niggle of unexpected anxiety rushing through her.

Flowers on her porch was one thing, but somebody watching her while she went about her daily business was something else. A chill threatened to walk up her spine as she went to her living room window and peered outside.

She flipped the blinds closed and then chided herself for being silly. She'd had on the pink tank top and had been around town all day. There was no reason to believe there was anything ominous about flowers on her porch or the sender's knowing she'd worn pink.

Still, as she moved away from the window she wondered if there was somebody out there now.

Watching her.

Chapter Two

It was an appropriate day for death and funerals. Bo woke just after eight to gloomy dark clouds obscuring any morning sunshine.

Although he'd been in bed and trying to find sleep, he was still awake when Jimmy came in just after three in the morning. Bo remained in bed, his brain whirling and refusing to shut off.

Memories of his mother had plagued him, and he dreaded both the service that day and the final act of packing up her things and giving them away. At least he didn't have to worry about what to do with the house right away. Jimmy had grown up on the swamp side of town, in one of the shanties that threatened to tumble down beneath a stiff breeze.

He and Bo had become best friends in third grade and Jimmy had spent much of his time at the Mc-Bride house, eating meals, staying as long as he could before he had to return to the shanty where his brutal alcoholic father lived with his verbally and mentally abusive wife.

As soon as Bo had opened Bo's Place, he'd hired

Jimmy to be his manager and Jimmy had finally escaped the swamp, moving into a small apartment in the back of a liquor store in the center of town.

When Bo realized his only chance to survive financially and emotionally was to get out of town, it was only natural that he turned to his best friend to move into the house Jimmy had always thought of as his real home. The benefit to Bo was that he knew Jimmy would take care of his mother so she wouldn't be all alone.

It had been a win-win situation for both of them and Bo was in no hurry to toss out the man who had played the role of son when he couldn't be here.

He now rolled out of bed and pulled on a pair of jeans, and then padded into the kitchen where he made coffee. As he waited for it to brew he remembered that just before he'd finally fallen asleep his thoughts had been filled with Claire Silver.

She'd been the first woman in two years who had caught his attention in any way, who had filled him with a touch of curiosity and an unexpected attraction.

She had eyes the color he'd always imagined the waters of the Caribbean might look like, an azure blue that appeared too beautiful to be real. They also had held a spirit that he wasn't quite sure was confidence or craziness.

He dismissed thoughts of her as he poured himself a cup of coffee and sat at the table. In the distance, through the gloom he could see the top of the ridge where new construction was taking place.

Large equipment had been brought in, indicating that whatever was going to be built up there was going to be big. Bo couldn't imagine what would stand on that property, but it didn't matter to him. He definitely wouldn't be here to see whatever it was completed.

He drank two cups of coffee, disappointed that apparently the sun didn't have the energy to burn off the dark clouds overhead. He only hoped that if it rained, it would wait until after the service that afternoon.

He returned to his bedroom where he made his bed and pulled his black suit from the closet. The last time he'd worn it had been to his father's funeral, and it was still encased in dry-cleaner plastic.

He removed the plastic and wondered how many people would show up at the cemetery. Brenda McBride had been well liked among her peers in the small town. But that had been before Shelly's murder. He'd hoped that by him leaving town she'd been able to keep her friends and hadn't been stigmatized by his presumed guilt.

By the time he'd laid the suit on the bed, he smelled the scent of bacon frying coming from the kitchen. He returned to the kitchen to find Jimmy standing in front of the stove, clad in a pair of khaki shorts, a white T-shirt and a pair of worn sandals.

"I didn't expect you to be awake yet," Bo said as he sat at the table.

Jimmy flashed him a quick smile. "I'm usually up just before eleven. I guess I don't require as much sleep as most people." He flipped the bacon strips. "Scrambled eggs okay?"

"Since you're cooking, whatever works for you," Bo replied. "I'm really not that hungry anyway."

"It's going to be a stressful day. You need to eat something," Jimmy said.

Bo didn't reply. Within ten minutes Jimmy set a plate of bacon, scrambled eggs and toast in front of him and then sat across from him with a plate of his own.

"What's going on up there?" Bo asked and gestured out the window to the top of the ridge.

Jimmy took a bite of toast and chased it with a swallow of coffee before replying. "Mayor Frank Kean was unseated in the last election and our new mayor is on a mission for Lost Lagoon to be found. The town sold the land on the ridge to some corporation that is putting in an amusement park."

Bo stared at him in surprise. First he was stunned to learn that Frank Kean had been voted out after serving as mayor for the past ten years or so. "An amusement park?" he finally said incredulously.

Jimmy nodded. "Jim Burns was voted in as mayor and you know what a hotshot he's always been. Once he was in office he surrounded himself with like-minded councilmen and then rallied the business owners to push through the sale of the land. There was one heated town meeting before the final vote. As you can imagine most of the old-timers didn't want to see the town overrun with tourists and the like, but there were enough who believed Lost

Lagoon is a dying town and the amusement park was the opportunity to get it prosperous and thriving."

Bo stared at his friend for a long moment, trying to digest what he'd just learned. "Why would anyone choose this place to put in an amusement park?"

Jimmy shrugged. "Rumor is it will be pirate themed to play off the legends of pirates once roaming the area."

Many of the businesses in town had already embraced the pirate theme years ago. There was the Pirate's Inn, rumored to be haunted by pirates who couldn't find their ship; the Treasure Trove sold pirate T-shirts and fake swords along with elaborate costume jewelry and gold-wrapped chocolate coins. On Main Street you couldn't walk ten feet and not see something pirate-related.

"Frank Kean must have been devastated to lose the election," he said.

"Actually, I think he was ready to step down. Besides, he's on a small committee that's working closely both with the city council and the people building the park. There are still some people disgruntled about the whole thing, but it's a done deal and life will definitely change around here when the park is done."

As they finished their breakfast Jimmy continued to fill him in on the happenings in town, who had gotten married and who had gotten divorced and all the rest of the local gossip.

Bo encouraged the conversation, knowing it was much easier to talk about things and people he didn't care about anymore than think about the service for his mother that afternoon.

After cleaning up the kitchen, it seemed all too soon that it was time to shower and get dressed for his final goodbye to his mother.

As he dressed in a white short-sleeved dress shirt and his suit pants, he thought about the fact that he hadn't mentioned to Jimmy his unexpected interaction with Claire Silver the night before.

Maybe he was afraid that Jimmy would tell him that Claire was nice, but was also the town's nutcase, and Bo liked her. He didn't want to hear anything negative about her. Right now she and Jimmy were the only two people in this godforsaken town he liked.

He doubted he'd see her again. Tonight he'd have Jimmy bring home some sturdy boxes from the bar, and tomorrow Bo would pack his mother's things, catch up with the lawyer, and by Saturday or Sunday be back on the road with Lost Lagoon just a distant memory.

Oh, he would forever be bound to this place because of his nearly lifelong friendship with Jimmy and his secret ownership of Jimmy's Place, but there would be no reason to ever come here again.

He carried his suit jacket into the kitchen and placed it across the back of a chair, and then walked to the window and stared outside as he waited for Jimmy.

It was two o'clock and outside the window the dreariness of the day remained unchanged, as if a reflection of Bo's somber mood. He already knew his mother had requested a closed casket and a short grave site service performed by Pastor Ralph Kimmel from the Methodist church she had attended for years.

The cemetery was only a ten-minute drive and Bo didn't see any reason to arrive too early. There was nobody he wanted to visit with and he suspected that few people would attend.

Jimmy walked into the kitchen, clad in a dark gray suit that Bo vaguely remembered once had belonged to him. Thankfully the two were about the same size, and many times over the years Jimmy had been given clothes from Bo.

"Maybe we should go ahead and head out. If we get there early you could at least have a few minutes alone before anyone else arrives," Jimmy suggested.

Bo nodded and grabbed his suit jacket and pulled it on, dread, grief and anxiety all boiling inside his stomach. His mother had grieved long and hard following the death of his father, and there was some consolation that the two of them were now together once again.

Minutes later they were in Jimmy's car and headed toward the Lost Lagoon Cemetery. With each mile Bo's heart grew heavier as emotion pressed tighter and tighter against his chest.

Once they arrived it was easy to see where the ceremony would take place. A small white canopy fluttered in the sultry air over the plain white casket, which was already in place to be lowered into the ground.

Nobody else was there yet, and as Bo got out of the car and walked toward the site the emotion in his chest rose up to blur his vision with tears.

He quickly brushed them away, not wanting anyone to see any weakness, but they appeared once again and he was grateful that Jimmy had hung back, giving him a moment alone.

He stood at the foot of the casket, his brain whirling with memories of his mother. She had been the one who had pushed him after high school to drive back and forth to the bigger city of Hattiesburg to attend college, where he'd received a business degree by the time he was twenty-one.

She'd then encouraged him to open Bo's Place, her and his dad fronting him the money to begin the successful venture. One of his proudest days had been when he'd been able to pay them back every cent of their seed money.

"So, I figured I hadn't seen the last of you." The familiar deep voice coming from behind him tensed every one of Bo's muscles.

He turned to see Sheriff Trey Walker and his deputy, Ray McClure. Both men had been Bo's biggest accusers and both had been extremely frustrated that they hadn't been able to put together a case that would see Bo in prison for Shelly's murder.

"What are you doing here?" Bo asked, unable to hide a hint of hostility.

"We always come out to pay respects to one of

our own," Trey replied, his green eyes narrowed as he held Bo's gaze.

"Maybe you should be spending this time looking for the person who really murdered Shelly," Bo said.

"Already know the answer to that question," Ray said. Ray was a mean little creep, built like a bulldog and as tenacious as one. He had been one of the loudest mouths proclaiming Bo's guilt in Shelly's murder.

Bo was about to tell the two of them to get the hell out of there when he heard a female voice calling his name. He watched as Claire ran toward them. Clad in a pair of slender black slacks and a white blouse, the sight of her immediately diffused some of Bo's anger.

She reached Bo's side and looped an elbow with his, as if presenting a united stance. At the same time Jimmy joined them along with Pastor Kimmel, who immediately took Bo's hand in his.

His faded blue eyes held a kindness that warmed him as much as Claire's surprising nearness and open support. "It's a sorrowful day when we have to say a final goodbye to such a good woman."

Bo nodded, unable to speak around the lump that had risen in his throat. Claire moved closer to his side, as if she sensed the myriad emotions racing through him.

Pastor Kimmel released his hand and stepped back, nodding to the other attendees. "Shall we get started or should we wait to see if others want to come to pay their respects?"

Bo glanced at the road by the cemetery. There

wasn't a car in sight and it was three o'clock. "Let's get this done," he said roughly.

So his mother would be sent off to her final destination by a pastor, a loving son, a surrogate son, two cops who thought her son was guilty of murder and a woman Bo hadn't decided yet if she was completely sane.

CLAIRE HAD A FEELING few people would be here today. Brenda McBride had become a semi-shut-in after Bo left town. She and Jimmy showed up every Sunday morning for church, but other than that she was rarely seen out and about.

The service was short yet emotional, and Bo's face and body radiated a soul-deep sorrow that Claire felt inside her heart. She didn't know what it was like to have a loving, caring mother, nor did she know much about having a decent father, but that didn't stop her from imagining the depth of Bo's loss. She'd felt the same way when Shelly had been murdered, that something precious and beloved had been stolen away from Bo.

When the service was finished, Bo looked hollow-eyed and lost. His jaw clenched as Trey and Ray approached him. "You planning on staying in town?" Trey asked.

"Why? Do you intend to put up posters of my face to warn young women?" Bo retorted. He drew a deep, weary sigh. "Don't worry, I just have a few things to clear up and I should be gone by the weekend."

"That's the best news I've heard all day," Ray said.

Claire saw every muscle in Bo tense as a red flush rose up his neck. "Come on, Bo. I'm taking you home with me," she said. Bo looked at her in surprise. "Jimmy, I'll bring him home later this evening."

She grabbed him by the hand and physically pulled him away from both the lawmen and his friend. He balked for only a moment and then went willingly with her.

They didn't speak as they walked through the cemetery and to her compact car parked in the lot. She got behind the wheel as Bo folded his long legs into the passenger side.

"You have a car," he said, stating the obvious.

Claire started the engine. "My usual mode of transportation around town is my bicycle, but I get the car out for special occasions and when the weather isn't conducive to riding or walking."

She felt his gaze on her. "Thank you for showing up today," he said. "And for stepping in before I punched Ray in his face."

"I figured you could use a stiff drink rather than a night in the jail," she replied. "Besides, Ray McClure isn't worth the effort of an uppercut. He's a weasel who likes to chase anything in a skirt and hand out tickets for looking at him cross-eyed."

"He was one of the loudest voices screaming my guilt all over town before I left," Bo said. Once again she felt his gaze on her, warm and intense. "What am I doing in your car going to your home?"

She flashed him a quick glance and then focused back on the outer road as they rounded the tip of the lagoon. "I figure within an hour or so Jimmy will be leaving to go to work, which means you'll probably be holed up in your house all alone, and nobody should drink alone."

"What makes you think I'm going to drink?"

"Because I would if I were in your shoes. You just buried your mother. I don't think you need to be by yourself right now."

"You're kind of a pushy woman," he replied lightly.

A small laugh released from her. "I'm sure I've been called worse. I hope you're a gin-and-tonic kind of man because that's what I've got at the house."

"Anything is fine," he replied, his voice suddenly weary.

She pulled up in front of her house in the driveway that just barely held the length of her car. "Home, sweet home." She unbuckled her seat belt and got out of the car at the same time as Bo.

"Nice," he said. "I don't remember this place looking like this. You must have put a lot of work into it."

She was acutely aware of his presence just behind her as she walked up the porch and unlocked the door. The hot, sultry air intensified the scent of him...a fragrance of shaving cream and pleasant woodsy cologne. "It took me a full year to get rid of what once stood here and make this a real home."

"Looks like you have a gift."

She turned and looked where he pointed to the edge of the porch, where a vase of flowers sat on a folded note. A wave of irritation swept through her.

If this was some sort of a charming courtship game it had gone on long enough.

She grabbed the vase and note and then ushered Bo inside. "Apparently I've picked up a secret admirer." She set the vase in the center of the table next to the one from the day before. "Take off your jacket and get comfortable." She gestured toward the beige sofa with bright green and turquoise throw pillows.

He took off his jacket and slung it across the back of one of the kitchen chairs. "Do you have any idea who your secret admirer might be?" he asked.

She pulled from a cabinet a large bottle of tonic and a bottle of gin, and then opened the refrigerator door to grab a couple of limes. "Not a clue," she replied. "And honestly I think the whole thing is ridiculous. If some man is interested in me, then he should just step up to the plate and tell me. Lime?"

"Sounds good."

As she cut up the limes he wandered the space, checking out the books on her turquoise-painted ladder bookcase, the green and blue knickknacks that she'd found to give the house a sense of home. He finally landed on the sofa. After handing him his drink, she sat on the opposite side of the sofa with her own.

"Why are you being so nice to me? Aren't you afraid somebody in town will see you with me and you'll be shunned?" he asked, his midnight-blue eyes holding her gaze.

She took a sip of the biting yet refreshing drink and then placed it on the coffee table in front of them. "I don't pay much attention to what people think about me. I'm often on the unpopular side of an issue." She offered him a sympathetic gaze. "You want to talk about your mother?"

He settled back against the cushion and took a long, deep drink from his glass. "Not really. I've had days to do nothing but think about her and now I'd much rather talk about you."

"Me? Trust me, there isn't that much to talk about. I was born and raised here. My mother ran off when I was six and I was left with a neglectful alcoholic father in a shanty that threatened to fall down whenever the wind blew. I went to college on a full scholarship and got my teaching degree. When I returned here my father had disappeared and I haven't seen him since. And that's my story."

She leaned forward and grabbed her glass and then took another sip. She'd made her drink light on gin and heavy on tonic and had made Bo's drink heavy on gin and light on tonic.

"So, your turn. Tell me what you've been doing for the last two years," she asked. "Have you made yourself a new, happy life? Found a new love? I heard through the grapevine that you're living in Jackson now."

He nodded at the same time the sound of rain splattered against the window. "I opened a little bar and grill, Bo's Place, although it's nothing like the original." His dark brows tugged together in a frown as if remembering the highly successful business he'd had here in town before he was ostracized.

He took another big drink and then continued, "There's no new woman in my life. I don't even have friends. Hell, I'm not even sure what I'm doing here with you."

"You're here because I'm a bossy woman," she replied. She got up to refill his glass. "And I thought you could use an extra friend while you're here."

She handed him the fresh drink and then curled back up in the corner of the sofa. The rain fell steadily now. She turned on the end table lamp as the room darkened with the storm.

For a few minutes they remained silent. She could tell by his distant stare toward the opposite wall that he was lost inside his head.

Despite his somber expression, she couldn't help but feel a physical attraction to him that she'd never felt before. Still, that wasn't what had driven her to seek contact with him, to invite him into her home. She had an ulterior motive.

A low rumble of thunder seemed to pull him out of his head. He focused on her and offered her a small smile of apology. "Sorry about that. I got lost in thoughts of everything I need to get done before I leave town."

"I wanted to talk to you about that," she said.

He raised a dark brow. "About all the things I need to take care of?"

"No, about you leaving town."

"What about it?"

She drew a deep breath, knowing she was putting her nose in business that wasn't her own, and yet unable to stop herself. "Doesn't it bother you knowing that Shelly's murderer is still walking these streets, free as a bird?"

His eyes narrowed slightly. "Why are you so sure I'm innocent?" he asked.

Claire had never had a problem speaking her mind or sharing her thoughts, but she found herself reluctant to truly answer his question, afraid that he'd think she was silly, or worse, the loony tune she already suspected he thought she might be.

"I'm three years younger than you and Shelly and I know it sounds crazy, but I was in love with your love for each other. You two were the shining example of what I wanted to find for myself someday. I watched you walking the streets, hand in hand, having ice cream outside the ice cream parlor."

The words tumbled out of her, as if the more she spoke the less he'd think she was nuts. "I saw the way you looked at her, Bo. I know the reputation you had in town as being a caring, gentle soul, a loving son, and I don't believe there was anything Shelly could have done that would have resulted in you hurting her."

Bo stared at her for a long moment, his eyes a darker shade of blue than she'd ever seen them. "Thank you," he finally said. "And of course it bothers me that her killer has never been brought to justice."

"It bothers me so much I carry pepper spray

everywhere I go," she said. "I try to be inside the house with the door locked after dark."

Bo took another drink, his gaze not leaving hers. "What does all this have to do with me leaving town?"

Claire uncurled from her position and moved closer to him. "I don't think you should leave town. I think you should stick around and prove your innocence."

Bo laughed, the sound deep and rusty, as if he hadn't laughed in a very long time. "You are out of your mind."

"I don't think so," she protested. "You know that at the time of Shelly's murder there wasn't really a thorough investigation. Law enforcement focused on you to the exclusion of anyone else."

"Shelly's case is a cold case that nobody is working because they all believe I did the crime. I can't imagine Trey or Ray agreeing to reinvestigate it just because I'm back in town," Bo said.

"You're right," she agreed. "They wouldn't lift a finger to help you with any unofficial investigation, but I would." She saw his dubiousness in his eyes and quickly pressed forward. "Think about it, Bo. We don't even know if the sheriff and his men interviewed any of Shelly's friends after her death. I don't believe they did much of anything, but you and I could talk to people, see what they remember about Shelly's life at that time, who might be a possible killer."

"It's a stupid idea."

"Maybe it is, but isn't it worth giving a little time to see what we might stir up? Wouldn't you like to prove your innocence to all the people who doubted you?"

Bo took a drink and sat forward. He placed his glass on the table and raked a hand through his slightly unruly hair. He glanced toward the window where the rain had stopped.

"I need to go home. You've got me half looped and considering things that shouldn't even enter my mind." He stood and she did the same, wondering what it might take to convince him that staying in town and fighting for his reputation would be worth it.

Of course, she'd spent years trying to convince her father to put down his bottle and be a real dad because she was worth it, and that certainly hadn't worked out.

Chapter Three

"Why not hang around a few weeks and see what you and Claire can dig up?" Jimmy asked. The two men were seated at the kitchen table eating ham and cheese sandwiches for lunch.

Already that morning Bo had met with his mother's lawyer, taken care of what paperwork needed to be done, and then had come back and packed part of the clothes in his mother's closet in the boxes Jimmy had brought home from the bar.

"If I know you, you've hired people at Bo's Place who are perfectly capable of running the business without you being present for a while," Jimmy continued.

Bo released a sigh. "I tossed and turned all night. The idea of staying here and putting myself through it all again isn't exactly appealing, and yet the idea of Shelly's killer still out there has haunted me for the last two years. I want to know who and I want to know why."

What he didn't mention to his best friend was how attracted he was to the woman who had put the idea in his head in the first place. He tried to tell himself that it was merely a combination of grief, gin and her proximity. But he'd wanted to fall into the depths of her amazing blue eyes, reach out and run his fingers through her curly mop of hair to see if the strands were as soft and silky as they appeared.

He had no idea what force had brought her into his life and why she was being so kind to him. Although she'd tried to explain her total belief in his innocence, he wasn't sure he understood her reasons. Still, the fact that he was innocent and she'd shown such belief in him had been a balm to a soul that had been scarred for two long years.

"How did you leave it with Claire last night?" Jimmy asked.

"She told me if I decided to stick around and become a crime investigation duo that she'd be hanging out at the school around two."

Jimmy nodded. "Coach Cantor has a key to the school, and I think once a week or so he and Claire sneak into the school gym and play one-on-one basketball."

"Coach Cantor?"

"Roger Cantor. He moved here about six months after you left. He's your typical jock type, but a nice guy." Jimmy looked over at the rooster clock on the wall. "That gives you about an hour if you intend to meet up with her at the school."

It was two thirty when Bo finally made up his mind and backed his motorcycle out of the driveway to head to the school. He was late so he wasn't even sure Claire would still be there, but if he didn't find her there he knew he'd eventually find her some- where. Or he had a feeling she'd find him.

It took him only minutes to arrive at the school, which housed students from kindergarten kids to seniors. Divided into two parts separated by a short breezeway, kindergartners through eighth were housed on the left and the right was for freshmen to seniors.

Claire's pink bicycle was locked to an old, rusted bike rack and a car was parked in the lot, letting him know that she and the coach were still here.

He parked his motorcycle next to the car and then headed for the front door of the high school side of the building. Locked.

He made his way around the side of the build- ing to the back where he knew there was a door that would take him into a hallway that led directly to the gym.

This door was unlocked, and as he stepped inside it was to the scents of pine cleaner and floor polish. Once school started again the clean smells would disappear beneath the odors of sweaty bodies and smelly gym clothes.

On either side of the hallway were doors that led to the boys' and girls' locker rooms.

Before he reached the gym he heard the sound of squeaky shoes pounding the floor and a male tri- umphant shout. He stepped up to the open doors and peered inside to see Claire facing off for a tip-off with a tall, pleasant-looking blond man who had the physique of a coach.

But it was Claire who captured his attention. Clad in a pair of white shorts that showcased shapely athletic legs and a turquoise T-shirt that clung to her feminine curves, she looked sexy as hell even dribbling the basketball, which had tipped to her side of the court.

She saw him and grabbed the ball in her arms, a warm smile curving her lips. She moved closer to him. "Bo, I didn't think you were coming."

"I wasn't sure myself until I got here."

She dropped the ball to the floor as the coach approached where they stood. Claire made the introductions between the two and Roger shook Bo's hand with a firm grasp and a pleasant smile.

"You play?" Roger asked and leaned down to pick up the ball. "I could use a little more competition to keep me in shape." He grinned at Claire as she started to protest. "Face it, Short Stuff, you're good for running me around, but not any real competition."

Bo smiled at the outrage on Claire's face. "Actually, I played a little in high school," he said. "But not since, so I probably wouldn't be any better competition than Claire."

"He wouldn't trade me in for somebody better," Claire replied. "If he had any real competition and got beat he'd go home and cry like a sissy baby. And speaking of going home, I've invited Roger back to my place for a late lunch, and now that you're here, you're coming, too."

"Oh no." Bo took a step backward. "I don't want to intrude."

"Nonsense," Roger replied. "It's an eat-and-run for me. Besides, Claire already told me she made chicken salad and you don't want to miss a chance to taste it. She makes the best."

Claire looped her elbow with Bo's. "No arguments. You're coming to eat and once we're finished you and I will have a chance to talk." Her blue eyes radiated a steely strength.

"You might as well just give in," Roger said. "When Claire makes up her mind about something it's darned near impossible to change it."

"Bossy little thing, isn't she?" Bo replied, making Roger laugh and Claire sputter a protest.

Minutes later as Bo followed Roger's car with Claire's bicycle fastened to a rack on its back bumper and her in his passenger seat, Bo realized Roger was right.

Claire was like a force of nature, a whirling dervish of focused energy. Cyclone Claire, he thought with wry amusement as he pulled up behind Roger's car in front of her house.

The moment they got inside the door, Claire pointed them to the table where the two men sat across from each other and talked about sports while Claire bustled to get plates and drinks on the table.

Bo almost immediately noticed two things about his male lunch partner. Roger appeared to be a nice man, and he seemed to suffer more than a little bit of obsessive-compulsive disorder.

Claire tossed his silverware next to his plate and he carefully lined up spoon, fork and knife and then moved his iced tea glass a half an inch to the right of his plate.

"We're rolling our own," Claire said as she placed first a large bowl of chicken salad in the center of the table and then a plate of soft whole-wheat tortillas next to the bowl. "Eat up," she said and joined them at the table.

Bo grabbed one of the tortillas and globbed the chicken salad onto it and then folded it into a semblance of a sandwich. Roger carefully spooned the salad into equal mounds and then rolled the tortilla into a neat burrito.

While they ate, the conversation remained pleasant. It was obvious Roger and Claire shared the camaraderie of coworkers and an easy friendship.

Once they were finished eating it took Claire only minutes to clear the table. "Have you asked Mary out yet?" Claire asked Roger as he got ready to leave.

He winced. "I haven't quite gotten up my nerve yet."

"You've been saying that for a month now. For goodness' sake, man, ask the woman out. She's a terrific woman and I'm sure you two would have a good time together," Claire said.

"I know, I'm working on it." With a wave of his hand to Bo, Roger thanked Claire for the meal and then left.

Bo sat back down at the table and after offering

him another glass of iced tea, Claire joined him. "He seems like a good guy," Bo said.

"He's a really nice guy," she agreed. "He's got some issues he's working on."

"You mean the OCD stuff?"

She raised a blond eyebrow. "So you noticed?"

"It was a bit obvious."

"Not as much as when he first arrived in Lost Lagoon," she replied. "His illness destroyed his first marriage, it was so out of control. He came here for a new start and he's been working with Mama Baptiste using herbs and meditation techniques to help him."

Everyone who had spent any time in Lost Lagoon knew Mama Baptiste. She and her son, Eric, lived two doors down from Claire and they ran an herb and apothecary shop in the center of town.

"Maybe Roger is your secret admirer," Bo suggested.

Claire laughed, the pleasant sound swirling that crazy warmth through him. "No way, Roger and I are strictly in the friend zone. He's got a major crush on Mary Armstrong, a waitress down at the diner, but as you heard he can't seem to get up the gumption to ask her out."

She waved a hand. "Enough about Roger." She placed her elbows on the table and leaned forward, her gaze so intent he felt as if she were somehow peering inside his soul. "So, are you in for a little crime investigation or are you out?"

The fresh, slightly floral scent of her perfume drifted across the table as her gaze continued to hold him captive. He had arrived at the high school not knowing what his decision was, whether he intended to hang around and buy into Claire's scheme of trying to find the real killer or get out of this town as fast as possible.

The light of her belief in him shone from her eyes. He bathed in it and realized he wanted this…his innocence restored among the people who had once been friends and neighbors.

"I'm in," he finally said. He hoped in making that decision he hadn't just made a mistake he would come to regret. Asking questions, talking to people and stirring up everything from the past also might stir up a killer's rage.

CLAIRE GRINNED AT Bo and popped up from the table to retrieve a pen, a legal pad and a three-ring notebook complete with color tabs from a kitchen drawer. "I hoped that was going to be your answer," she said as she once again sat down.

"What's all this?" Bo asked as he gestured toward the notebook.

"I'm a teacher, Bo. I love lists and notebooks and any kind of office supplies."

"You don't have any flash cards stuck in there, do you?" he asked wryly.

She laughed. "No flash cards, I promise." She was pleased that he'd decided to stick around and do a little digging into the crime that had forced him to leave town under a cloud of suspicion. She was also pleased that he apparently had a sense of humor.

She placed the legal pad in front of her and pushed the notebook to the side. "I figured we'd spend some time this afternoon coming up with a plan, names of people to talk to, the events that led up to Shelly's body being found in the swamp, anything that might provide a clue as to who was responsible for her death."

Bo raked a hand through his hair and leaned back in his chair. "It's a bit overwhelming, trying to go back to a crime that happened two years ago."

"Overwhelming is trying to keep second graders focused enough to learn math and reading," she replied. "This is just a puzzle and we need to start at the beginning and work outward. I know Shelly was murdered around eleven thirty at night. I don't know if I ever heard where you were at that time?"

When the murder had happened Claire had been as horrified as anyone in town, and although she'd tried to stay up on all the developments, she'd heard so many stories it was difficult to discern truth from false gossip.

"I was in my bedroom at my mother's house in bed with a twenty-four-hour flu bug."

"Then your mother was your alibi?" she asked and watched a growing darkness take hold in his eyes.

"An alibi easily dismissed. My mother was an early-to-bed kind of woman and she was also a woman who didn't lie." He raised his chin, obviously proud of his mother. "When Trey Walker asked her if she would know if I left the house that night after she went to bed, she confessed that she probably wouldn't have known."

"And there was nobody you saw or talked to who could confirm that you were in bed sick?"

Bo shook his head. "I went to bed a little after five. I made two calls before I crashed out, one to Freddie Hannity, who managed the bar at Bo's Place, to tell him I wouldn't be in that night and to take care of things for me. The other was a text to Shelly telling her I was sick and wouldn't meet her that night."

He paused a long moment, his eyes no longer dark blue but rather black and unfathomable. "You know Shelly was the night manager at the Pirate's Inn and night was my busiest time at Bo's Place. She started her shift at midnight so every night around eleven I'd sneak out of the bar and we'd meet at the bench down by the lagoon."

Once again he stopped talking and stared outside the front window, as if reliving each and every moment of that fateful night.

Claire had known that going back in time to the night of Shelly's death would be difficult for him, but she hadn't expected the rawness of his emotions. Even though Shelly had been gone for two years, it was obvious that love for her, that grief for her, still filled his heart.

Without giving it any thought, she reached out and covered his hand with hers. He blinked twice and then directed his attention to her hand. He turned his over and grasped her.

"Sorry, I got lost in my head." He gently extricated his hand from hers. "Anyway, the next thing I knew it was five in the morning and Sheriff Walker and Deputy Ray McClure were pounding on the front door.

"They told me Shelly had been killed around midnight and I needed to come into the station and answer some questions. I knew the minute I saw the way they looked at me that they believed I was responsible. I scarcely had time to grieve before I was vehemently defending my innocence."

"What did they tell you about the actual crime scene? I know Shelly was found in the lagoon, but she wasn't killed in the water." Claire picked up her pen, knowing that from this point forward the conversation would contain things she wanted written down. She didn't even want to think about how warm, how right it had felt to momentarily hold his hand.

He sat up straighter in his chair, his eyes once again focused. "The sheriff believed the actual strangulation occurred in the bushes around the bench and then she was put in the water, probably in hopes she wouldn't be found until morning or maybe forever. The bushes were trampled as if a struggle had happened, and they found her necklace tangled up in some of the brush. Her engagement ring was missing and has never been found. A couple of teenagers had gone to the swamp to gig for frogs. They're the ones who found her just after two."

"Why would Shelly have gone down there knowing that you weren't coming?" Claire asked. "Are you sure she got your text?"

"Positive. She texted me back that she'd see me the next day. As far as why she went to the lagoon that night, I have no idea. That question has haunted me for two years. I keep thinking that if I hadn't been sick that night...if I'd shown up as usual..." He allowed his voice to drift off.

"You can't blame yourself for this," Claire protested.

He raised a dark brow. "But apparently a whole town could blame me."

"That's because a real investigation was never done, and that's why we're doing this now," Claire replied. "I'm assuming your phone records were checked. How did Trey explain the fact that the texts were the last communications you two had that night?"

"He figured I'd found Shelly somewhere in town and didn't need to use any other form of communication."

"Did Shelly mention to you anyone who was giving her trouble? Anyone she'd made angry?"

"No, she didn't mention anything like that to me. Shelly wasn't the type to make enemies."

"Maybe it was something she didn't feel comfortable talking to you about. Maybe she'd have been more apt to confide in a girlfriend. Names, I need names of the people Shelly was closest to other than you," she said.

"Definitely Savannah."

Claire knew Savannah was Shelly's sister. She was a year younger than Shelly and the two had appeared very close. She wrote down Savannah's name on the legal pad. "You know she's now working the night shift at the Pirate's Inn. Who else can you remember?"

"Shelly was friendly with Julie Melbourne. I know they often had dinner together at Bo's Place while I was on duty. She also ran around with Valerie Frank and Sally Bernard. I think that's about it as far as her closest friends."

"Talking with Sally and Julie shouldn't be a problem. They're both teachers and I'm friendly with both of them. Valerie works the dinner shift at the diner. We can catch up with her there."

Bo scowled. "None of those women will want to talk to me."

Claire offered him a bright smile. "And that's why you have me. You'll be with me, but I'll do the talking." She looked outside where dusk had begun to fall. "We'll start first thing in the morning and try to get Sally and Julie interviewed. Then we'll catch up with Valerie and Savannah later in the evening."

He tilted his head and gazed at her curiously. "Do you really believe anything will come of all this?"

"All I know is that nothing will come of this if we don't try. I believe in your innocence, Bo, and I hate the fact that somebody got away with murder while you have carried this burden for so long. As far as I'm concerned you have two choices—stay here and work the case to prove your innocence or climb back on that hog of yours and leave town with that same burden weighing you down for the rest of your life."

He picked up his glass and peered inside it. "You didn't drug my drink, did you? Because when I listen to you, when I look into your eyes, I feel hope and I have to admit that scares the hell out of me."

"Embrace your hope, Bo." She desperately wanted to grab his hand again, to feel the warmth of his big grasp around her much smaller hand, but she knew it wasn't her place.

She was his partner in crime-solving, one of few people who believed he had nothing do with Shelly's death. She wasn't his girlfriend. She had a feeling Shelly still occupied that space in his heart, that she might always be there, allowing nobody else in for love.

For the next hour or so they talked about the elements of the crime, and Claire took copious notes that she would later transcribe into neat colored tabs of material in the larger notebook.

It was just after seven when Claire popped a frozen pizza into the oven, and once it was finished baking they continued their conversation while they ate.

They moved on from discussing the crime and Shelly to Bo's life in Jackson. "Bo's Place is small compared to what I had here," he said as he reached for a second piece of the pepperoni pie. "I don't socialize with the customers like I did here in Lost Lagoon. I keep pretty much to myself. I don't want people getting too close. It's easier that way…safer."

And it was the saddest thing Claire had ever

heard. Before the murder Bo had been gregarious and bigger than life. He'd made Bo's Place popular by his mere presence.

"And lonelier," she said softly.

Bo shrugged. "There are things worse than being lonely." He gazed at her curiously. "Why don't you have a boyfriend?"

"You mean other than my secret admirer?" she asked drily and then continued, "I dated Neil Sampson for about two months and then broke up with him six months ago. He's a city councilman and a nice guy, but there weren't any sparks, at least on my end."

"How did he take the breakup?"

"Not particularly well." Claire took a drink and thought about Neil. He'd shown little passion except for town business until she'd broken up with him, and then he'd spent the next month trying to talk her back into his arms.

"Is it possible he's your secret admirer?"

"I suppose it's possible," she replied thoughtfully. "But we've really had very little contact for the last five months or so. He's one of the liaisons between the town and the company putting in the amusement park and we really don't run in the same circles."

"And nobody else since Neil?" he asked.

"No. I'm twenty-five years old and as of yet I just haven't felt the kind of passion or love to bind my life with anyone." Except gazing into Bo's eyes definitely shot a tingling electricity through her that she tried desperately to ignore.

"You and Shelly dated for about ten years or so. Why didn't the two of you ever get married?"

"I asked her three times after we'd finished college and Bo's Place was up and running. Although she told me she was completely committed to me, she also told me each time that she wasn't ready to take the final plunge."

"Do you know what held her back?"

He frowned thoughtfully. "She didn't like her job at the Pirate's Inn. She was trying to figure out what she wanted to do...to be, and I think until she settled that she just wasn't ready to be my wife."

"They say on dark moonless nights her ghost walks along the edge of the lagoon."

Bo raised a brow. "Have you seen this ghost?"

"Not personally, but I know people who swear they've seen her. And some nights there are swamp lights that they believe is her spirit."

"And you believe all this? In ghosts and spirit lights?" There was bemusement in his eyes now, making him all the more attractive.

"I believe anything is possible," she replied. "I believe in angels and aliens, ghosts and goblins, all in both human and otherworldly forms."

"I knew I'd thrown my cards in with a nut," Bo teased.

Claire laughed. "This is Mississippi and we are a superstitious bunch."

They finished up the pizza and by that time darkness had fallen outside and Bo prepared to leave. She walked him to the door. "I know you still have things you're doing at your mother's house. Why don't we plan on me picking you up tomorrow right after lunch and we can start hunting down people and asking questions then?" she suggested.

"Don't you think it would be better if I just stayed home and you asked all the questions and then told me the answers?"

Claire smiled at him, but shook her head negatively. "That's not how partners work. Besides, I think it's important that people see you around town and that they know you're here to clear your name. You might be surprised to find out you still have friends here, people who never believed you were guilty."

"It definitely didn't feel that way when I left town," he replied.

She placed a hand on his strong, muscled forearm. "It's going to be different this time, Bo. We're going to find out the truth." She pulled her hand away, finding the feel of his warm skin far too pleasurable.

He opened the door and with a wave of his hand disappeared into the darkness. The low, guttural growl of his motorcycle filled the air as she turned on her porch light just in time to see him pull away from her house.

She automatically checked her porch, grateful to find no surprise gifts or notes, and then closed and locked her door and turned off her porch light.

She returned to the table and began to transcribe the notes from the legal pad into appropriate tabs in the larger notebook. Behind the red tab she listed all the people they intended to question the next day.

When that was finished, she moved to the sofa and thought about the conversation she and Bo had shared. It was obvious that the experience of being the number-one suspect in Shelly's murder case had changed him.

The old Bo had eyes that always held a wealth of openness, of warmth and welcome. The old Bo had believed that strangers were just friends he hadn't met yet.

This new Bo wore his wariness in the shadows that filled his eyes, in the defensive tension of his body, although she'd seen glimpses of the old Bo in his wry humor and his cautious and surprising trust in her.

Angels and aliens, ghosts and goblins, she knew they weren't looking for anything or anybody supernatural or otherworldly.

She was looking for two men, hopefully one benign and one malevolent. She hoped to discover that her secret admirer was just some shy man in town who had yet to get up his courage to declare his interest in her. There was no reason for her to believe there was anything scary or threatening about flowers on her porch, she told herself.

The other man they sought was a cold-blooded killer, a man who had throttled Shelly Sinclair to death and then had tossed her body into the swampy lagoon like a piece of trash.

There was no question that she and Bo were about

to shake things up. She only hoped they shook out the real killer and saw him behind bars. They had to do this before Bo got discouraged and decided to leave town once again with the burden of his presumed guilt still riding his shoulders like a heavy leather jacket.

Chapter Four

Bo carried a third box of clothing from his mother's bedroom to the garage and tried to clear his mind of the dreams he'd entertained all night long.

For a year following Shelly's murder he'd suffered terrible nightmares, all of them with Shelly screaming his name, begging for him to help her, and him unable to stop her senseless death.

During the past year or so his sleep had been dreamless, but last night it hadn't been Shelly who had haunted his slumber, it had been Claire.

Claire with her tousled golden curls and achingly blue eyes, he'd dreamed of her in his arms, her body warmth heating all the cold places that had filled his for what felt like forever.

He dropped the box on the floor in the garage and told himself the dream had been driven by nothing more than the fact that Claire had offered him a friendly smile and a level of support he hadn't had before. Surely that was the only reason he'd entertained the erotic dream.

They were partners and nothing more, and would

remain partners until he decided to leave town, and this time when he left he would never be back again. Oh, he'd still talk to Jimmy on a regular basis, not only because Jimmy was a lifelong friend, but also due to Bo's silent ownership of Jimmy's Place.

"Need some help?" Jimmy poked his head out of the door that led from the kitchen to the garage.

"No, I think that's it for today." Bo checked his watch. "That gives me time to eat some lunch before Claire comes by to pick me up around one."

He joined Jimmy in the kitchen and headed for the refrigerator to pull out cold cuts for the noon meal. Jimmy sank down at a chair at the table. "Do you really think it's a good idea for you and Claire to go off like the Lone Ranger and Tonto to crime solve?"

Bo finished making his sandwich, knowing that Jimmy had eaten earlier. He sat down across from Jimmy before replying. "I don't know if it's a good idea or not. Hell, I don't even know if I'm the Lone Ranger or Tonto. Claire is running the show at this point. She has a touch of bossy in her, but at this point I'm willing to let her take the lead. I've been gone for two years and she's been here. All I know is that it's easy to get caught up in her optimism and there's no question I want the real killer identified and justice served."

"And I want that, too. But it's been so long. I can't imagine what you two will manage to dig up after all this time," Jimmy replied. "But it would be great if you could finally clear your name and get the real bad guy behind bars."

Justice for Shelly—hopefully if he and Claire could accomplish that then he would finally find some peace as he moved forward with his life. Shelly would always be a painful part of his past, but he knew that some of that pain could be released if her real killer were found.

"I'll say one thing, you've picked a good partner," Jimmy said, interrupting Bo's thoughts. "Claire is not only well liked, but she's also got a reputation as being a straight shooter who doesn't take any crap from anyone."

Bo couldn't help the smile that attempted to take hold of his mouth. "She seems like a bit of a fire-cracker."

Jimmy laughed. "That's Claire."

"I have a favor to ask you," Bo said, thinking ahead. "I know you use Mom's car. Could you park outside from now on? There's plenty of room on the driveway for my motorcycle and the car, and that will give me space to stack all the boxes of Mom's things."

"Not a problem," Jimmy agreed.

Minutes later Jimmy drifted back to his bedroom and Bo finished his sandwich, trying not to think about the woman who had haunted his dreams, a woman he'd found himself drawn to since the moment she'd tossed him a to-go bag of burger and fries.

He didn't want to be attracted to her. He didn't want to be attracted to anyone. Losing Shelly had been devastating, but the aftermath of her murder had been nearly as devastating as he'd watched close friends and good neighbors turn against him.

His trust in people had been shattered and thick defenses had built up around his heart. He'd learned in the past two years that being alone wasn't such a bad thing.

He spent quite a bit of his time at Bo's Place, overseeing the daily operation. In his spare time he often took long drives on his bike, allowing the wind in his face to blow out any thoughts of past, present or future.

In the lonely hours of the night when he might have been making love to a woman, he often read books on business or history, or the occasional adventure novel.

He'd grown comfortable…safe in his loneliness and he wasn't about to let some curly-haired cutie under his skin. Still, at one o'clock when he slid into the passenger seat of her car, a nervous energy twisted in his stomach.

He told himself it had nothing to do with the sky-blue blouse she wore that clung to her breasts and enhanced her eyes. It had nothing to do with the fresh, floral scent of her that filled the car. The jumpy tension was the result of what they were about to begin today…talking to people who believed he'd murdered his girlfriend.

She frowned at him as he settled in. "I should have told you to wear something else."

He looked down at his black jeans and T-shirt and

then gazed back at her. "I didn't know there was a dress code for the day."

"A white or blue shirt might have been better. You look dark and brooding."

"Like a bad guy," he replied.

She flashed him a quick smile. "Ignore me, I'm probably overthinking things."

It was hard to ignore her when a vision of his dream from the night before flashed through his head. He consciously willed it away. "So, who's first on your list to talk to?" he asked and noticed that her yellow legal pad was shoved down in the space next to her seat.

"I thought we'd start with Sally Bernard."

Bo nodded and braced himself for a face-to-face meeting with the tall redhead who wasn't shy about speaking her mind. He'd once considered Sally a friend of his as well as of Shelly's, and Sally and her boyfriend had often come to Bo's Place for their evening meal.

Sally had been one of the first of Shelly's friends to turn on him and he definitely wasn't looking forward to seeing her again.

They passed the street where Shelly had lived. "Are Craig and Margie still living in the same place?" he asked.

"They left town about six months after Shelly's death. I heard they moved someplace up north. Mac and Savannah stayed together in the house until about eight months ago when Mac got married and bought his own place."

Mac was Shelly's older brother. He would be thirty-two years old now, and the last time Bo had seen him Mac had sworn if he got the chance he'd kill Bo.

"Then Savannah lives in the home alone now?" he asked.

Claire nodded. "She doesn't date and pretty much keeps to herself. Of course, working the overnight shift at the Pirate's Inn isn't exactly conducive to dating."

"I always thought of her like a little sister." A wave of sadness swept through him. "With her being just a year younger than Shelly, sometimes it was hard to get the two apart." He looked at Claire. "She's definitely somebody you should talk to alone. I don't want to be there when you question her."

Claire turned into Sally's driveway, cut the engine and took off her seat belt. "We'll try to catch up with Sally, Valerie and Julie as soon as we can, then I'll drop you back at your house and find Savannah and talk to her."

Bo released a small sigh of relief, grateful that she seemed to understand his reluctance to question Savannah. "And after you talk to her, you can head back to my place for dinner and tell me what she had to say," he said.

"Sounds like a plan," she agreed. "Now, are you ready for this?"

Bo unfastened his seat belt and looked at the small house where he and Shelly had visited occasionally for barbecues and card games. "She hasn't gotten married?" he asked, knowing he was stalling for time.

"Hasn't even come close in the last couple of years. She dates occasionally, but nobody in particular." Claire narrowed her eyes slightly. "Do you want to sit out here and discuss Sally's love life or do you want to get out of the car and see what she might know about Shelly's life before she was murdered?"

Bo drew a deep breath and opened the door. "Let's get this done," he stated with a renewed burst of nervous energy.

As they headed up the walkway that led to the front porch, Bo wondered if this all wasn't a fool's errand. He could finish packing up the last of his mother's things in another day and be back on the road to Jackson. He could put all this behind him, but instead here he was, about to pick the scab off old wounds.

As if she read his thoughts, Claire smiled at him, that crazy warm smile that shot heat through him. "You're doing the right thing, Bo. You deserve the truth. We all do, and this is the first step in finding out that truth." She knocked on the door.

The tall, slender redhead answered with a bright smile that immediately fell into a scowl as her blue eyes gazed at Bo. "Claire, what are you doing on my doorstep with this murdering slimeball?"

"Don't worry, Sally. I left all my homicidal tendencies at home this morning," Bo replied drily and then grunted as Claire delivered a sharp elbow to his ribs.

CLAIRE WANTED TO pinch off Bo's ears. She wanted to give him a sobering slap. The last thing she needed from him was defensive sarcasm. "Bo and I would like to ask you some questions about Shelly."

"She's dead. What's to ask?" Sally made no effort to open her door wider to invite them inside.

"Do you want to do this here on your front porch where all of your neighbors can see, or can we come inside? It's important, Sally."

Sally hesitated a moment and then with a deep, audible sigh opened the door to allow them entry. She gestured them toward her sofa and then sat in a chair across from them, her gaze focused solely on Claire.

"I know you believe that Bo is guilty of Shelly's murder, but he's not," Claire began. "He and I are looking for any information that might point to the real killer."

"And why don't you believe it's not Bo? Because he told you so?" Sally asked with a touch of sarcasm.

"He's not in jail. There was never any real evidence to point to his guilt except for the fact that he and Shelly were a couple. There was never really an in-depth investigation into the murder. Bo was the focus and I don't believe anyone in law enforcement looked anywhere else," Claire replied.

Sally crossed her arms, obviously in defensive mode. "So, what do you want from me?"

"You and Shelly were good friends. Was there anyone bothering her or angry with her before her death that she might have mentioned to you?" Claire asked. Bo shifted positions next to her and leaned forward.

"Not that I remember. The only person Shelly told me she ever argued with was Bo."

Claire fought her urge to look at the man seated next to her. Was there something he hadn't told her about his relationship with Shelly? Had they not been the golden couple Claire had always thought them to be?

"Are you sure there wasn't anyone else who had issues with Shelly?"

"Not that she ever mentioned to me." Sally unfolded her arms. "But I'll confess Shelly and I were social buddies, not necessarily heart-to-heart confidantes. You might talk to one of her other girlfriends, or Savannah. They might have known more about stuff that was going on in Shelly's life than me."

"Well, that was a waste," Bo said moments later as they got into Claire's car.

"Not necessarily," Claire countered. "She's a name we can now cross off our list. Besides, she said it was possible some woman closer to Shelly might know more."

Claire backed out of the driveway and headed in the direction of their next stop. "What's this about you and Shelly arguing?"

Bo sighed and leaned his back against the headrest. "Shelly and I never had huge arguments, but we did have an ongoing difference of ideas that grew bigger over the last year before her death." He sat up straighter and ruffled his hand through his hair. "Shelly wanted to leave Lost Lagoon and move to a bigger city. She wanted me to sell Bo's Place and start all over someplace else. Business was booming, I felt like my mother needed me here, and I loved life in Lost Lagoon. I wasn't willing to give it all up. I believed that if Shelly and I got married and had babies, she'd be happy here, and if she needed more than that, I encouraged her to get involved with the city council or to go back to school."

"Is that why she wouldn't marry you?"

"She never actually told me that, but yeah, I think that was the reason." He gave a dry laugh. "It's ironic that only after her death did she get her wish and I left everything behind to move to a bigger city."

It was ironic and it was tragic, Claire thought. "Did you and Shelly have a particularly public argument in the days before her murder?"

"No, nothing like that. In fact, it didn't come up that often. It wasn't like we argued about it every day. It was more like a discussion we had every couple of months. Losing faith in me?"

She cast him a quick glance. "Not at all, I'm just trying to understand all of the dynamics."

"The truth of the matter is I don't think Shelly and I would have ever married," he said, his voice softer. "I think eventually she would have left Lost Lagoon and me behind."

"You're shattering the image I had of your romance with Shelly. During my teenage years I'd see you two together and then go home to my shanty where my father might or might not be there and I'd dream about finding a love like yours and Shelly's.

To be honest, that idea got me through a lot of difficult times."

Her cheeks warmed as she realized she'd shared more than she'd meant to with him. She didn't like to think about her childhood or the loneliness she'd felt as a motherless child whose father was gone more than he was at home.

If it hadn't been for Mama Baptiste she would have never made it to school on time and would have gone to bed hungry on many a night.

"Maybe Julie will have something to tell us," she said to break the silence that had descended between them.

"Let's hope. Somebody had a beef with Shelly, something was happening that I didn't know about. It wasn't a random act. She wasn't robbed except for her engagement ring, and it certainly wasn't anything spectacular. Her purse was on the bench, with her wallet and cell phone inside."

"Do you know if the police checked pawn shops to see if anyone tried to pawn the ring?" she asked.

"I don't know what the police did except crawl all over me and try to find the evidence to put me in jail for her murder," Bo replied. "But as far as I know the ring was never recovered."

"Maybe the murdering creep kept it as a souvenir," she replied and fought a shiver that threatened to crawl up her spine.

"And that sounds like some sick obsession," Bo replied. "The police found nothing on Shelly's cell phone or her laptop that would lead to another suspect, and I never noticed anyone lurking around whenever we were together. My text was the last thing on her phone, no more incoming calls or texts after that."

"Somebody wanted her dead for a reason, or somebody met with her that night and somehow things got out of control. Did you ever consider that the killer might be a woman?"

She sensed Bo's look of surprise. "It would take a strong woman to strangle Shelly."

"Rage can give somebody plenty of strength, and Shelly was a petite, slender woman."

"I just never considered a woman as a suspect. I can't imagine her making that kind of a female enemy. Like I told you before, I can't imagine her making any enemies."

Claire pulled into the driveway of Julie Melbourne's home and then turned to look at Bo. "Did you feel somebody stalking you before Shelly's death? Have any women who were showing an interest in you?"

"And killed Shelly out of some kind of jealousy?" He shook his head. "I don't remember anyone flirting or acting inappropriate with me. Everybody in town knew that Shelly was my fiancée and I was committed to her."

"It was just a thought," Claire said. "Now let's hope Julie has something more tangible for us than Sally had."

Unfortunately, Julie had nothing for them. She was obviously surprised and not particularly happy to see Bo, but she invited them in and the conversation went nowhere. No, Shelly hadn't mentioned anyone bothering her before her murder. She hadn't talked about anyone who was angry with her or making her uncomfortable.

"You're wasting your time on me," Bo said once they were back in the car and headed to his house. "We're not going to find any answers."

"Are you really ready to quit after talking to just two people? I don't know about you, but I'd much rather be doing this than serving up George's greasy burgers," Claire replied. "The pay isn't as great, but the company is definitely better. Besides, maybe Savannah knows something that will move us forward."

"That would be good," he replied. She pulled to the curb in front of his house.

"Let's hope she's home," Claire said as Bo opened his car door. "I'll catch up with her somewhere and be back here in an hour or so. If I run into a snag I'll call you." They exchanged cell phone numbers.

"And I'll have some dinner ready when you get back here."

"Sounds good," she replied. She watched as he got out of the car and headed toward his front door. He looked defeated and she had a feeling it wouldn't take much for him to cut and run.

It was three thirty when she parked her car at her house, deciding to walk to Savannah's place and then on to Bo's. She felt the need to stretch her legs. Her mind always seemed to clear when she walked or rode her bicycle, and she wanted to think about what she wanted, what she hoped to hear from Savannah.

It didn't take her long to reach the Sinclair home, where Savannah answered the door on Claire's first knock. As always when Claire saw Savannah she thought of Shelly. The two sisters looked so much alike with their long dark hair, delicate features and wide brown eyes.

"Sally called me earlier so I've been half expecting you," Savannah said as she gestured Claire into the house. "Bo isn't with you?"

"We thought it would be best if I talked to you alone," Claire said as she sat on the chair Savannah gestured her to in the tidy living room.

"Sally told me you were asking questions about before Shelly's murder." Savannah sat on the sofa and curled her legs beneath her.

"I'll be completely honest with you, Savannah. I never believed that Bo murdered Shelly. I also don't believe an adequate criminal investigation was conducted at the time of her death," Claire said.

Savannah raised her index finger to her mouth and nibbled on her nail, her doe-like gaze never leaving Claire's. She dropped her hand into her lap and released a deep sigh. "I never really believed in Bo's guilt, either."

The confession shocked Claire. She leaned forward in the chair, a sizzle of excitement rushing through her. "Was there somebody else you suspected? Did Shelly mention anyone bothering her in the days or weeks before she was killed?"

"No, nothing specific, although she did tell me she was dealing with a potentially sticky situation and was trying to figure out how to handle it. But she refused to tell me any more than that."

Claire frowned. "A sticky situation? What could that possibly mean?"

"I don't know, but I'm pretty sure it didn't have anything to do with Bo. I know that she and Mac were fighting, but Mac would never hurt Shelly. Trust me, over the past two years I've tried to figure out what she might have been talking about. I wished I'd pressed her for more details, but I didn't, and I don't know if it had anything to do with her murder or not."

"What were Shelly and Mac fighting about?" Claire asked curiously.

"Who knows? They were always fighting about something. Sometimes Mac took his role as protective older brother too far and Shelly got aggravated with him."

"Why did you have doubts about Bo's guilt?" Claire asked, filing away in the back of her mind Mac as a potential suspect.

"Bo had been a part of my life since I was fifteen. I loved him like a brother. I knew how much he loved Shelly, and through their years together I never saw him lose his temper. In fact, Shelly used to complain that Bo didn't like to fight, that he never lost his cool."

"Why didn't you come forward on his behalf after the murder?" Claire asked.

Savannah's eyes darkened. "Everyone around me seemed so certain it was Bo and nobody had an alternative suspect. My parents were devastated, my brother Mac was in a rage and my best friend, my sister, was dead. I was in no condition to say much of anything to anyone. As time went by everyone just seemed to forget it. Bo was gone, Shelly was dead and I thought I just needed to move on with my life until I heard Bo was back and the two of you were asking questions."

"I believe Bo is innocent, and he and I believe somebody got away with murder that night and has never faced justice. We're determined to find out who was really responsible for Shelly's murder."

Claire stood, eager to let Bo know that Savannah had always had doubts about his guilt. She knew the information would lift his spirits.

Savannah walked her to the door. "You'll let me know if you think of anything that might help Bo and me try to find the killer. Needless to say we don't expect to get much help from the local law enforcement."

"I'll call you if I think of anything that might help, but I've been thinking about this for two long years and haven't come up with any answers." Savannah opened the door. "Please tell Bo that I was sorry to hear about his mother's death. She was a wonderful woman."

Minutes later Claire walked the sidewalks that

would eventually lead her back to Bo's house. Despite the fact that she'd learned nothing concrete, she was filled with a new optimism brought on by learning that Savannah had believed Bo was innocent. Other than Shelly, Savannah would have known Bo's character better than anyone.

A sticky situation—what could that mean? What kind of a situation had Shelly been facing in the days before her death? Had she had issues with a coworker at the Pirate's Inn?

Had she become enamored with another man and the sticky situation was that she was conflicted between her love for Bo and a new romantic interest?

As she walked, her mind whirled, darting first in one direction and then another. It was just after four and the hot, humid air wrapped around her like an oppressive blanket, making her wish she was in the air-conditioning of her car.

It was only going to get worse. The summers in Mississippi were brutal, especially in the couple of months to come. By the time July came she wouldn't be walking or riding her bicycle anymore until cooler fall weather set in.

She was almost to Bo's house when a new thought struck her. Had Shelly received a note from a secret admirer? Had she found a little vase of flowers on the porch before her death?

Despite the heat that surrounded her, a shiver slid up her spine. "Don't be silly," she muttered aloud. There was absolutely no reason to tie what had happened to Shelly Sinclair two years ago to the notes and the flowers Claire was receiving now.

Still, she hurried her pace to Bo's, the chill inside her refusing to relinquish its hold.

Chapter Five

As soon as Claire dropped Bo at his house, he pulled a package of steaks out of the freezer, scrubbed a couple of large baking potatoes and then sat at the kitchen table to think.

He'd gone into today not expecting answers, not expecting anything but rather indulging Claire and her crazy idea to clear his name. He'd decided he'd spend a couple of days "investigating" and then head home to Jackson.

Talking with Shelly's friends, Sally and Julie, had only made him more discouraged. After all, it had been two years. Did Claire really expect to solve a crime that the police had probably officially moved to a cold case status, but unofficially had declared solved?

Certainly Bo would like to know who was responsible for Shelly's murder. He wanted to see that person behind bars, but the odds of him and Claire managing to do that after all this time and with no official help were slim to none.

Jimmy was in the bedroom dressing for his night

at Jimmy's Place and Bo took the opportunity of the quiet time to call his manager in Jackson.

The call didn't take long and, as expected, everything was running smoothly. Bo had made a great choice when he'd hired Art Bolling as his manager. The forty-five-year-old man was not only honest and hardworking, but he was also a good leader who all the workers respected. It put his mind at ease that he had good help while he was away.

Jimmy came into the kitchen, his lanky frame clad in black slacks and a black shirt sporting Jimmy's Place in white lettering. He smelled like a bottle of cologne and had his brown hair slicked back with gel. "The chick magnet is ready for duty," he said with a grin.

"Is there any chick in particular in the magnet's sights?" Bo asked in amusement.

"Nah, right now I'm just spreading the wealth of my charms all around." He straightened his collar and frowned. "I was dating Maggie Grimes for a little while. Remember her? She sat in front of me in algebra class when we were sophomores."

Bo had a vague memory of a cute redhead with big green eyes. "What happened?"

"I figured out she was just dating me for the free drinks she could get at the bar. She liked being my girlfriend at Jimmy's Place but she wasn't much into me outside of that." He shrugged. "Plenty of other fish in the sea and I'm in no big hurry." He checked his watch. "And on that note, I'm out of here."

Once Jimmy had left, Bo scrubbed the potatoes,

poked them with a knife, then covered them with aluminum foil and set the oven to preheat. It was funny, he'd thought he'd become accustomed to the relative silence in his life over the past two years. But in the past two days Claire had filled that silence and he found himself looking forward to her arrival no matter what information she had learned.

He was torn between the decision to stick around and move forward with her in an effort to prove his innocence, and just heading out and leaving Lost Lagoon forever behind.

He was still contemplating what he wanted to do when Claire returned. Her energy bounced off the walls as she greeted him and followed him into the kitchen.

"Savannah never really believed in your guilt," she said with a smile before taking a seat at the table.

Bo's knees nearly weakened as he moved across to the oven to put the potatoes inside to bake. Sweet Savannah, she'd always held a special place in his heart as Shelly's younger sister.

"She also said to tell you she's sorry about your mother's passing," Claire continued. Bo joined her at the table.

"Did she have any information that might be useful to us? Anything that might shed some light on things?" he asked.

She filled up the room with her presence, instantly dispelling the oppressive silence, the thrum of loneliness that had beat in his heart moments earlier.

"Nothing specific, but she did say just before

Shelly's murder Shelly had mentioned that she was dealing with some sort of sticky situation."

Bo frowned. "Sticky situation? What does that mean?"

"I have no idea and Savannah didn't know, either, but I think if we can figure it out it's the key to the murder."

"How exactly do we go about figuring out something like that?" Bo asked in exasperation. "It could have been an issue at work or a fight with her brother. It might have been unwanted attention from somebody or an issue with a girlfriend."

"And step by step we'll explore all those things," Claire said, her voice calming the storm of frustration that threatened to erupt inside him.

"Why wouldn't she have told me about something bothering her?" Bo asked, speaking more to himself than to Claire. He'd thought that he and Shelly shared everything with each other, both good things and bad. Had she possessed secrets that led to her death?

Claire seemed to know that his question had been rhetorical and she didn't attempt to answer it. In fact, she changed the subject as he got up to season and then broil the steaks. She chatted about teaching and how much she loved spending time with her second-grade class. "They're old enough to know the school routine, but also have a wonderful innocence and eagerness to learn that's so rewarding."

As she regaled him with stories about some of the funny antics of some of her students, Bo felt himself relaxing…enjoying the sound of her laughter and the fact that she could make him laugh so easily when levity had been missing from his life for so long.

The easy conversation continued throughout their meal. He told her a little bit more about Bo's Place in Jackson and the small rental house he called home. He considered telling her that he still owned Jimmy's Place, but ultimately decided not to. It really didn't matter. He had no plans to remain in Lost Lagoon and publicly reclaim his place at the popular bar and grill.

"Jimmy definitely has taken on his role as owner of Jimmy's Place well," Claire said with a touch of humor. "He was always kind of quiet and introverted, but now he's like you were when you were running the place. He's gregarious and something of a social butterfly."

"I'm just glad he's happy. He had a crappy childhood. He was raised in one of the shanties near where you live. Both his parents were alcoholics who either beat him, verbally abused him or ignored him. But from what little you've told me, it sounds like your childhood was pretty crappy, too."

"It wasn't great," she admitted and dolloped more sour cream on her potato. "My mother left when I was six years old. I went to school one morning and when I got home she was gone and she never came back. My father was already a drinker, but after she left he fell into the bottom of a bottle and never crawled out. He was gone more than he was home and when he was home he was usually passed out."

"How did you survive?" Bo asked, his heart swelling with empathy for a little girl who'd apparently had nobody to nurture her.

"On hopes and dreams and with a lot of help from Mama Baptiste, who stepped in to make sure I made it to school and had a good breakfast before starting the day."

"But she had her store to run—she couldn't be there all the time for you."

"True. I spent a lot of time alone, but I had a wonderful second-grade teacher who taught us all that we decide if we're happy or sad in most situations. She explained that it was okay to be sad, but eventually we each had to find our own happiness."

A dainty frown line appeared across her forehead, not detracting from her prettiness in any way. "I have to confess, it took me a while to understand that the true path to happiness was in acceptance."

"I'm not sure I understand," he replied, holding her gaze for so long he felt as if he could drown in its blue depths.

"When I realized my mother wasn't coming back, that she'd not only left my father but also me behind, I was devastated." Her eyes shimmered and Bo reached across the table to cover one of her hands with his.

Having been raised in a good stable home with both a mother and father, Jimmy's and Claire's backgrounds not only seemed alien, but broke his heart for each of them.

"I couldn't understand how my mother could just leave and start a new life somewhere and not take me with her. It took me almost a year to realize and accept that she was gone and she wasn't coming back and I was strong enough to be happy despite my circumstances."

Bo squeezed her hand and then released it. Even though she appeared to have gotten past her childhood, he knew there had to be some scars left behind.

It was after they'd finished eating and cleaned up the kitchen that the conversation turned back to the investigation.

"I think tomorrow we should head over to the Pirate's Inn and talk to Donnie Albright," Claire said.

Bo knew Donnie was the owner of the Pirate's Inn. With a long beard and wiry thick gray-and-white eyebrows, he looked like one of the pirates who purportedly haunted the hotel.

"After that we'll try to find more of Shelly's friends out and about and talk to them, and then we'll end up at the diner for dinner where Valerie is working and we can speak with her," Claire said.

The task ahead of them felt daunting. "I should have stayed," Bo said and slapped his palms down on the table in frustration. "I should have stayed here after Shelly's murder instead of running away. I should have forced Trey Walker and his men to do a real investigation. Dammit, I should have never left town with my tail between my legs."

Regret and more than a little self-disgust swept through him. It would have been so much easier to find out the truth two years ago.

"If I remember right, you didn't have much of a

choice except to leave town. Your business was virtually boycotted, cutting off your financial support, and you also had no emotional support except from your mother and Jimmy," Claire reminded him.

"Mom was most of the reason I did leave. She encouraged me to get out of town and hoped that eventually the true killer would be found. I finally agreed to leave because I thought life would be easier on her if I wasn't here. I thought maybe she'd be able to continue to live a normal life, that people would support her, but you saw at her funeral that she was obviously ostracized anyway."

He swallowed his bitterness and glanced toward the window, surprised to discover that darkness had fallen. "You'd better get home before it gets any later," he said.

Claire glanced toward the window and frowned, then turned back to look at him. "Would you mind taking me home? I walked here and I really don't feel comfortable walking home alone in the dark."

"Of course I'll take you home," he replied. "I don't want you walking home alone at night. I've got an extra helmet in the garage. Let me grab it and we'll head out."

Minutes later they were on the Harley, Claire's arms wrapped tight around his waist and her thighs pressing intimately against his.

Desire for her heated his blood, a desire he'd had to tamp down every minute he spent with her. He had a feeling she felt the physical chemistry between them, as well.

But he had no intention of pursuing anything romantic or sexual with her. There was no point. He was on a mission to seek a killer, and once that mission was accomplished he would return to Jackson alone.

He was almost sorry when they reached Claire's house and she climbed off the back of the bike. She handed him the helmet and he hung it on a clip near the back of the bike.

"Why don't we plan on me picking you up around ten in the morning?" she suggested.

He nodded, and then noticed a white piece of paper that appeared to be taped to her porch railing. "Looks like you got another note from your secret admirer." He pulled off his helmet and got off the bike. He followed behind her and watched as she pulled the note off the railing, read it and then handed it to him.

In the bright moonlight overhead it was easy to read the bold black block letters. STAY AWAY FROM BO MCBRIDE. "Is it the same writing as your secret admirer?" he asked.

She took the paper back from him with a shrug. "Hard to tell. It could just be from somebody who doesn't like the fact that we're asking questions." She wadded it up and smiled. "Don't worry about it. I'll see you tomorrow at ten."

He waited until she disappeared into her house before getting back on his bike and taking off. Restless energy filled him, an energy that made the idea of going back home unpleasant. On impulse he headed for Jimmy's Place. The dinner crowd would have moved out by now, leaving the place to the social drinkers and partiers.

It was Saturday night and the place was packed. Bo pulled around to the back of the building and parked. He wasn't looking for trouble, he just had a desire to sit and drink a beer in the place he owned.

He went in through the back door, which led him to a storage area that held a set of stairs and metal rows of shelving. He went through to the kitchen where two cooks worked, but neither of them spoke or stopped him as he walked on. He passed down the hall with the restrooms and then into the main area.

The long polished bar was just to his right and a single bar stool sat empty at the edge. It was rarely used as it was separated from the main row of bar stools that lined the front of the bar. The only person who had sat there regularly had been Shelly on nights she came in before work and Bo was behind the bar.

He slid onto that stool now, grateful that, for at least the moment, nobody had noticed his arrival. The bartender, an older man he didn't recognize, worked the opposite end of the bar where a couple of young women sat.

When he'd finished serving them he scanned the bar area and noticed Bo. Bo ordered a beer and once it had been served, he swiveled slightly in his chair to look around.

Jimmy stood at a table where four people were

seated, obviously playing goodwill ambassador as he smiled and clapped one of the men on his back.

It should be me, Bo thought. *I should be the one greeting people and thanking them for coming in.* He turned back around and took another drink of the cold brew.

There was no going back in time. He'd made his decision to leave and put Jimmy in control so that the place would continue to survive. Certainly his ownership allowed him to reap financial benefits, but he mourned the position in his community that he'd lost in the process.

Bo was almost finished with his beer when Eric Baptiste walked by him, apparently headed for the restrooms. He took several steps down the hallway and then turned back and stepped up close to Bo.

Eric was two years older than Bo and while the two had never had any problems, they had not been close friends. Eric leaned a muscular arm on the bar next to Bo and gazed at him with flat black eyes.

"About Claire," he said softly.

"What about her?" Bo asked.

"If you hurt her in any way, I'll kill you." Eric didn't wait for a reply, but turned on his heels and disappeared down the hallway.

Bo drained the last of his beer and threw enough money on the bar to cover it, then got up and left the way he had come. As he drove home he wondered if perhaps Eric was Claire's secret admirer?

All he knew for sure was that he'd felt a malevolence wafting off the muscular dark-haired man.

Was his warning really about Claire or did Eric Baptiste have something deeper to hide…something like murder?

Chapter Six

Claire knew the last place Bo wanted to be on a Sunday night was in the diner where the crowd was thick and they had to wait for a table to be cleared in Valerie Frank's area.

When they were finally seated, she knew he couldn't help but notice the people at most of the tables around them whispering and pointing in their direction.

She was proud of the straight set in Bo's broad shoulders, in the way he carried himself as if he had as much right to be in this town, in this diner, as anyone…which he did.

"I'm starving," Claire said as she picked up the menu on the table in front of her.

"That's the gnaw of frustration you're feeling," Bo replied drily.

It had been a day of frustration. They'd started by visiting with Donnie Albright at the Pirate's Inn. Donnie hadn't been able to shed any light on what was going on in Shelly's life before her murder, nor had anyone else they'd spoken to throughout the afternoon.

"Tomorrow is another day," she replied optimistically. "Right now all I can think about is a big plate of meat loaf, mashed potatoes and a hot buttered roll."

"All I can think about is that treasure chest in the Pirate's Inn lobby that Donnie was painting that tacky gold," Bo replied.

She laughed. "Upgrades for the crowd of tourists he's hoping the new amusement park will eventually bring to town, and he's not the only person who is making changes and updates to their businesses."

"I can't imagine Lost Lagoon being filled with tourists." Bo closed his mouth as Valerie approached their booth, her eyes widening slightly at the sight of him.

"Hi, Valerie, how's it going?" Claire said lightly, as if it were ordinary for her to show up for dinner with the local bad-boy suspected murderer.

"Okay." Her brown eyes slid a quick glance at Bo. "I heard you were back in town."

"Valerie, I didn't kill Shelly and I decided it was finally time for me to come back to find the real killer. Claire has been helping me do the investigation that the cops never did two years ago." Bo held her gaze. "We wondered if you knew about anything or anyone that was bothering Shelly before her murder?"

"Or maybe why she went to the lagoon that night when she knew Bo wasn't meeting her there," Claire added.

"I don't know why she was at the lagoon," Valerie

said. She glanced around, as if worried she was spending too much time at their table. "She seemed preoccupied in the days before that night, but when I asked her if something was bothering her, she told me it was something she had to work through on her own. Look, I need to get to my other tables and that's really all I can tell you. So, what would you like to drink?"

After taking their drink orders, she hurried away from the booth. "I wonder if the sticky situation was me," Bo said. "Maybe she had finally made the decision to leave me and head out of town and was just waiting for the right moment to tell me."

"That possibility doesn't upset you?" Claire asked.

He smiled and warmth shot through her. He had a beautiful smile and she wished she'd see it more often. "During the last six months of our relationship I began to accept the fact that Shelly and I probably weren't going to have a happily-ever-after together. Although we both pretended things were fine, there was a bit of a strain between us, and I knew it was because Shelly wasn't happy here."

"But we can't know for sure that you were her sticky situation. That's just speculation and we can't take it as fact," she replied.

Valerie returned with their sodas, took their meal orders and then disappeared once again from their booth. Claire sipped her soda and tried not to focus on how utterly hot Bo looked.

Riding on the back of his motorcycle last night had filled her with a sexual charge. She'd molded her legs against his muscular ones, wrapping her arms around his taut middle and pressing herself so close to his back, and it had stirred up a desire to yank him off the bike and take him into her bedroom and make love.

Unfortunately, the note that had awaited her had stanched any feelings of lust. Although she'd made light of it in front of Bo, the note had kept her sleepless for half the night.

Had it been from her secret admirer? Was it a warning of some kind? Or had it simply been a concerned friend or neighbor who didn't want her putting herself at risk by hanging out with a "murderer?"

"So, what's our next move?" Bo asked, pulling her from her thoughts.

"It would be nice if we could get the murder book from the sheriff to see exactly what kind of investigation was done before."

Bo laughed, the sound rich and bold and once again stirring a heat inside her. "There is no way Sheriff Trey Walker would even let us get close enough to spit on the files of Shelly's case. Remember, officially it's still an open case."

"Was there anyone working the case who didn't seem to be completely closed-minded about looking at other suspects?"

Bo frowned thoughtfully. "At the time it certainly felt like every deputy on the force was determined to find evidence to put me away, but now that I think about it there were two deputies who seemed open to other possibilities."

"Are they still in town working as deputies?"

"I know one of them is—I saw him in a patrol car yesterday, Deputy Josh Griffin. The other deputy was Daniel Carson. I haven't seen him since I've been back so I don't know if he's still around or not. The little interaction with them that I had was definitely less confrontational, and they appeared to be more open to other alternatives of the crime."

"Then we need to talk to them," Claire replied. The conversation halted as Valerie returned with their dinners.

"I don't think they'll talk to us." Bo picked up the conversation as Valerie once again left them alone. "Sheriff Walker is a tough bully with his favorite sidekick of Ray McClure. I'm sure both Griffin and Carson would be concerned about their jobs if they were to speak to us about the case."

"Enough shop talk," Claire said as she picked up her fork. "Let's talk about something else while I wallow in this mound of mashed potatoes and gravy."

Bo grinned. "Definitely a meat-and-potatoes kind of girl?"

"You've got that right. Leave the rabbit food to the bunnies."

"Shelly ate rabbit food," Bo said as he cut into the chicken-fried steak he'd ordered. "She always ordered salads when we went out and complained if I encouraged her to eat other food or have dessert. I thought all women worried about their weight like she did."

"Not me," Claire replied. "I guess I have a good metabolism and I've never had to worry about gaining too much weight." She spooned a bite full of creamy potatoes into her mouth, swallowed and then continued, "To be honest, I remember far too many nights going to bed hungry, so I enjoy food now whenever I get the chance."

Bo's gaze was soft as he looked at her from across the table. "I hate the thought of your childhood. It breaks my heart that you went to bed hungry and were so alone."

"There were lots of us swamp kids who didn't have the perfect life, but we managed to survive," she replied. "You mentioned to me that Jimmy had a pretty rotten start to life."

"True, but he had me and my family to help him. I gave him clothes and shoes and we fed him when he was hungry and my mother tried to comfort him when he was scared." Bo smiled. "From third grade until now, Jimmy has always been my brother from another mother."

"I hope Jimmy knows how lucky he was," Claire said.

"I consider myself just as lucky. He's been the best friend I could ever have."

They quieted for a few minutes, each focused on their food. Claire glanced around the diner, grateful that the initial stir that had occurred when they'd walked in had died down and nobody seemed to be paying them any attention.

Meanwhile she found herself far too focused on Bo. Despite the savory fragrances that floated in the air, she could also smell the scent of Bo's woodsy cologne.

She knew better than to get emotionally or sexually involved with him. They were partners and had become friends while working on a crime, but it would be foolish to cross over a line into anything more intense.

Her life was here in Lost Lagoon, and she had no idea how long he'd commit to being here. His life was now in Jackson with the new Bo's Place, and there was really nothing to keep him here long-term. She wasn't even sure he'd stay long enough to get the answers to clear his name, although he appeared fairly committed at the moment.

They were halfway through the meal when Neil Sampson walked in with Mayor Jim Burns. The mayor headed for the counter where apparently a take-out order awaited him while Neil stopped at their booth.

"Claire," he said, completely ignoring Bo's presence. "You're looking as lovely as ever."

And you're looking stuffy and pretentious. Thankfully the words flew only in her head and not out of her mouth. "Thanks," she replied. "Have you met Bo?" she asked.

Neil's gaze never left hers. "No, and I don't have

any desire to. I just wanted to stop and say hello to you. I often think of our time together."

"I would think you'd have a lot more important things to think about," she replied, irritated by his rudeness with Bo.

He stepped back. "I just wanted to say hello."

"And so you have," Claire replied.

Thankfully by that time the mayor motioned to him from the door and with a final nod of his head, Neil hurried toward the exit.

"I'm assuming that was your ex. He seems like a nice guy," Bo said drily.

"He's an ass. He wasn't as bad before he became Mayor Burns's number-one lackey, but power and position have definitely transformed him, and not in a good way."

"It sounds like he still cares about you. Maybe he's your secret admirer," Bo suggested.

"Doubtful. That's not really his style, but who knows." She shook her head to rid it of thoughts of her secret admirer. She didn't want to think about that mystery right now. She still believed eventually her admirer would come out of the woodwork and confess his feelings for her.

By the time they finished their meal and lingered over coffee, dusk had fallen outside. "Why don't you go and start the car and get the air-conditioning running while I pay the bill," Bo suggested.

"Sounds like a plan to me," she agreed. Even though the June sun had gone down, it would still be hot and sticky outside.

She stepped out into the thick humidity and pulled her keys from her purse as she focused on her car parked across the street.

She stepped off the curb and had only taken a couple of steps into the street when she heard the roar of an engine and the squeal of tires against hot pavement.

She was halfway across the street when bright headlights flashed on from a car careening toward her. She froze, her mind unable to comprehend that she stood directly in the path of death.

It took Bo an instant to recognize the imminent danger to Claire when he stepped outside. He didn't think, he simply reacted. He leaped from the curb and when he was close enough he lunged at Claire, the momentum of his speed catapulting them to the other side of the street where Claire slid up to the sidewalk one way and he rolled the other way.

He'd felt the heat of the car engine, still smelled the scent of burning rubber and oil in the air. He remained unmoving for a long moment, his breath stolen and his brain frozen by the near-death experience they both had just endured.

His head cleared and mentally screamed Claire's name. He rolled over to see her pulling herself up to a sitting position, a stunned expression on her face.

Ignoring pain in his hip and elbow, he rose to his feet and rushed to her side. "Are you okay?" He crouched down beside her, hoping he hadn't broken any of her bones with his tackle.

Her knees were bleeding and raw, as were the palms of her hands. Still, she got to her feet. "I'm okay. A little bruised and battered, but…" Her voice trailed off and in the waning light of deep twilight, tears suddenly sparkled in her eyes. "What just happened?"

Bo quickly pulled her into his arms, bloody knees and all. She clung to him for a long moment, her body radiating the heat of adrenaline and the coldness of fear.

She pulled back and he reluctantly let her go. "You probably have gravel in your knees and hands. We need to get you to the doctor," he said.

"I don't need a doctor," she replied and quickly swiped away any remnant of tears. "All I need is my purse. I've got some tissue inside that will clean up the blood." She looked around and spied it not far from where she'd fallen.

Once she'd grabbed it, Bo gestured her to the passenger side of her car and he got in behind the steering wheel. "And now we're going directly to the sheriff's station."

"Why? I just want to go home." Her voice held the heaviness of tears ready to be shed.

He hesitated a moment, wondering if he should soft-pedal what had just occurred. Instead he decided to be painfully honest. "We need to talk to Trey because somebody just tried to kill you."

He felt the weight of her stare. "Surely you're mistaken. It had to have been a drunk driver, or somebody who just didn't see me in the road. Why would anyone want to kill me?"

Good question, Bo said to himself. But he couldn't deny the fact that the car didn't swerve in an effort to miss her, that brakes hadn't been applied to stop the terrifying forward movement of the car.

"I'd just feel better if we report what happened to Trey," he said.

She opened her purse and pulled out several tissues and cleaned off her palms and knees as best as she could without the aid of water. "Maybe the driver was on his cell phone and got distracted for a minute," she said, still looking for answers to explain away what had just occurred.

"Maybe." Bo didn't want to push the issue and upset her even more than she already was.

They remained silent for the rest of the short ride to the sheriff's station. The station was a one-story building and as Claire and Bo walked into the small reception area they were greeted by Betsy Rogers, who worked as both receptionist and dispatcher.

"We need to talk to Sheriff Walker," Bo said.

"He's in his office. You can go on back," Betsy replied.

Bo placed an arm around Claire's shoulder as they walked by the desk where Betsy sat and pushed open the door that led to the squad room. There were a total of eight desks and only Deputy Josh Griffin was present at one, apparently doing paperwork.

He glanced up at them as they walked toward the back of the room where Trey's glass-enclosed office was shrouded in secrecy by closed blinds along the front.

Bo didn't bother knocking. He dropped his arm from around Claire's shoulder and opened the door to reveal Trey leaned back in his chair with his feet propped up on his desk and Ray McClure slouched in the chair in front of him.

"What the hell?" Trey pulled his feet off the desk and sat up straight in his chair. Ray remained in place, an obvious show of disrespect to both Bo and Claire.

"Somebody just tried to run over Claire in the middle of Main Street in front of the diner," Bo said. "If you get somebody over there now there should be witnesses."

Trey motioned Ray up. "Take Josh with you and see what you can find out," he said. Once Ray had left the office, Trey gestured Claire into the empty chair. She sank down and Bo stood just behind her, a hand on her shoulder. "Now, tell me again, in detail, what happened."

"Claire and I ate dinner at the diner and when we were finished, while I paid, she went outside and headed for her car, which was parked across the street," Bo said and then continued to explain the car that had seemingly come from nowhere aimed directly at Claire. As he spoke he felt a small shudder move through Claire.

Trey's gaze softened slightly as he looked at Claire. "I can't imagine anyone in this entire town wanting to hurt you, Claire." His gaze hardened and shifted to Bo. "But I can think of plenty of people who might want to run you down. In fact Mac Sinclair was in here just yesterday complaining about your presence back in town. Are you sure that car wasn't aimed at you?"

Had he been farther into the street than he'd thought? Had it been the intention of the driver to swerve at the last moment and strike him? Bo just didn't know.

"Maybe it was some drunk coming from Jimmy's Place, or some stupid teenager drag racing down the street," Trey added. "But I can't imagine Claire being the target of whatever happened out there tonight."

"It doesn't matter who the target was," Bo countered. "That car almost killed Claire."

"What color was the car?" Trey asked.

Claire looked up and back at Bo, and then gazed at Trey. "I have no idea. All I saw were bright headlights."

"It was dark…black I think." Bo frowned. "I was a little busy getting Claire out of the way to pay attention."

"So, I'm guessing you didn't get a plate number," Trey said.

"That would be a good guess," Bo replied. It had been stupid to come here, he realized. They had no real information to give to Trey in order to identify the vehicle and no idea of anyone who might want to harm Claire.

"I'll write up a report and we'll see if Ray and Josh can find a witness who might be able to give us more information. Other than that, there's nothing much else I can do."

"You'll let me know if they find out anything?" Bo asked. "I'll give you my cell phone number." When that was completed, he squeezed Claire's shoulder. "Come on, let's get you home where we can properly clean up your hands and knees."

She didn't hesitate. She popped out of the chair as if she couldn't wait to leave. There was no question she was still shaken up. Her face was unusually pale and her eyes appeared larger than usual.

Once again Bo took the driver's seat while she slid into the passenger side. "We'll take you to my place and get you cleaned up," he said.

"No, just take me home, Bo. I want to be home. You can drive the car back to your place and pick me up tomorrow," she replied. Bo turned around and headed in the direction of her home.

"Maybe it was just some stupid drunk," she said. "Or a reckless teenager racing down the street." Her own words seemed to calm her.

"Or somebody who intended to swerve at the last minute to hit me," he added. "I know I have a target on my back with some of the people here in town, but like Trey said, I can't imagine anyone wanting to hurt you. I've seen the way people react to you. You're a favorite among everyone."

"I don't know about that, but I would be hard-pressed to come up with anyone who would want to see me dead," she replied.

By that time he'd pulled to the curb in front of

her house. He got out of the car, ignoring the fact that with each passing minute his body was radiating with more aches from his violent tumble across the street.

He could only assume that Claire was feeling the same thing. By tomorrow they would both be dead-tired.

He walked with her to her front porch, where she unlocked her door and turned back to him. "Thank you for saving my life, Bo."

"If you think you're getting rid of me that quickly, you're mistaken." He pushed past her and into her living room. "Since you didn't want to go to the hospital to take care of your hands and knees, I'm assuming you must have a first aid kit of some kind around here."

"I can take care of it. It's not necessary for you to do it," she protested.

"I say it's necessary," he said firmly. "I've let you be boss of this partnership long enough."

Her eyes widened. "I haven't been bossy," she exclaimed. He raised one of his brows and her cheeks grew pink. "I've just been organized and had a plan each day."

"Right now I'm the one with the plan. Now, where are your first aid items?"

"Under the cabinet in the bathroom." She closed and locked the front door and led him to the bathroom just off the living area. He went directly to the sink and began to run the hot and cold water, turning the faucets until he was satisfied with the temperature.

He then turned to where she stood just behind him and moved her in front of him, wrapping his arms around her. He took her wrists and held her hands under the running water.

For a moment he was nearly overwhelmed by the feel of her warmth and curves so close to him and the sweet, fresh scent of her hair. He steeled his mind and focused on the task at hand. He was grateful to see that as the dried blood slowly left her palms, there were only minor scrapes that wouldn't even require any bandages.

Once her palms had been cleaned, he motioned her to sit on the commode so he could attend to her bloody knees. He used a warm washcloth to gently remove the blood, once again grateful that he found no grit or gravel embedded in her skin.

After washing both knees, he applied antibiotic cream to them and then topped each with a bandage that sported a happy face. He gently kissed each bandage and then rose to his feet. "Boo-boos not only cleaned but properly kissed," he said lightly.

She looked up at him with new tears shimmering in her eyes. "I've always wondered what it would be like to have somebody kiss my boo-boos," she said at the same time a soft sob escaped her.

In a flash of memories, Bo thought of every night his mother had tucked him into bed with a good-night kiss, how many times she'd fixed a boo-boo with a gentle press of her lips. He'd taken for granted all of it, and the thought that Claire had never had anyone to tenderly tuck her into bed or kiss away the pain of a scratch or scrape broke his heart.

He pulled her to her feet and into his arms, wanting to kiss every wound she'd ever suffered in her life, needing to be her soft place to fall that she'd never had as a child.

She clung to him, and when she raised her head to look at him he slanted his lips against hers. He meant the kiss to be soft and soothing, to comfort and calm after the trauma she'd suffered.

However, the moment he tasted her velvet-soft lips, he was lost. It was impossible to keep the kiss sweet and simple as she tightened her arms around his neck and opened her mouth to him in invitation to deepen the kiss.

He accepted the invitation, his tongue swirling with hers as his blood fired through his veins. The instantaneous desire that flared inside him shocked with its intensity and unexpectedness.

She must have felt it, too. She dropped her arms from around his neck and stumbled back from him, one hand reaching up to touch her own lips. "You should be boss more often," she said.

He'd love to kiss her again. He wanted to kiss her until they were both mindless with desire, eager to fall into bed together, but he didn't.

Despite her light words, she looked exhausted and

battle-weary. Now wasn't the time to do anything but encourage her to get a good night's sleep.

He reached out his hand and took hers and led her out of the bathroom. There was only one door in the house he hadn't been through and it was that door he opened… The door to her bedroom.

"What you need more than anything right now is to get into your pajamas and get some sleep," he said, even as his gaze swept the room that he would have instantly identified as belonging to her.

The walls were a pale gray, but the bedspread was an explosion of electric-blue flowers on a gray background, giving the room vibrancy. A vase of fake blue and yellow flowers sat on the nightstand, along with a yellow-based lamp.

Once again he was struck by the fact that when she'd renovated the old shanty into her home, she'd chosen bright, cheerful colors for every space.

"I'm going to get out of here and I'll lock up on my way out," he said.

"What about tomorrow?" she asked and sank down on the edge of her bed.

"I'll pick you up around eleven."

"But I haven't had a chance to plan what we need to do," she said.

"Don't worry. I'm playing boss again tomorrow and I'll have a plan. Now, get into your jammies and get some sleep." He left the bedroom and had just opened the door to leave the house when she called his name.

She stood in the bedroom doorway. "Just for your information, I don't sleep in jammies. I always sleep naked." With these surprising words, she closed her bedroom door.

Chapter Seven

The car careered toward her, the bright headlights blinding her as the acrid scent of burned rubber and hot oil filled her head. Then she was airborne, knowing that when she fell to earth death awaited her.

Death was her shanty where she shivered beneath her favorite blue blanket on a thin mattress on the floor. Outside the thin plywood walls she heard the slap of a creature in the water and feared that creature would creep in the darkness and through the slats in the wall and eat her.

Claire awoke with a gasp and sat straight up in the queen-size bed. Sunshine poured through the single window, and a glance at her clock told her it was just after nine.

She normally didn't sleep so late, but she'd had trouble going to sleep the night before. First she'd played and replayed through her mind that moment of being frozen as the car had headed directly for her, then she'd been plagued with thoughts of Bo's kiss.

Oh, that kiss. She drew in a tremulous breath and

fell back against her pillow, remembering the fire, the absolute mastery of his lips against hers.

She couldn't lie, she'd wondered what it might be like to be kissed by Bo, but there was no way her imagination had been able to conjure up how hot, how utterly breathtaking it would be.

She shouldn't think about it. She'd watched Shelly and Bo together for years and had dreamed of finding what she believed they'd found in each other. She'd believed they'd been each other's happily-ever-after and they might have been, had Shelly not been murdered.

Claire wanted that happily-ever-after for herself. She wanted that special man who loved her as desperately as she loved him. And she knew in her heart that man wasn't Bo.

Bo would have already been gone from Lost Lagoon if she hadn't talked him into hanging around for a while to try to find the real killer.

She had a feeling that with each day that passed with no answers about the murder, Bo moved closer to heading out of town. She didn't want him leaving behind her broken heart.

She got out of bed, grabbed her robe and pulled it around her, then padded into the bathroom and stared at her reflection in the mirror. It was as if she expected the imprint of Bo's lips to still mark hers.

Her mouth looked normal, no sign of the earth-shattering kiss they'd shared the night before. "It can't happen again," she said aloud to her reflection.

She started the water in the shower stall and once

it was a warm temperature she disrobed and stepped beneath the spray. She could not allow Bo to kiss her again. If he did she'd want more, and then her heart would spiral out of control. She had to keep her physical distance.

After showering she dressed in her usual fare of a pair of shorts and a sleeveless blouse. She took off the bandages on her knees, satisfied to see that the scrapes had already begun to scab over. It wouldn't be the first time in her life that she'd sported scabby knees or elbows.

She ate toast and drank a cup of coffee and scanned the names of the people they'd spoken to so far. She wrote notes and frustration niggled at her as she recognized they had really discovered nothing that moved them any closer to the truth of what had happened at the lagoon two years ago.

The irony wasn't lost on her that she wanted to do everything in her power to help clear Bo's name, but in doing that she was also helping him move on from Lost Lagoon.

At a few minutes before eleven she stood at her front door waiting for Bo to arrive to pick her up. She wondered what he had planned for the day. Although Lost Lagoon was a small town, there were still plenty of people to talk to who might have known something about the murder, somebody who could unravel the mystery of Shelly's "sticky situation."

The one person she didn't want Bo to speak to or have anything to do with was Mac Sinclair. Shelly's older brother was known to have a volatile temper, especially since the murder of his sister. The fact that he'd already contacted Trey to do something to get Bo out of town indicated his continued hatred for the man he believed murdered Shelly.

She hated the way her heart lifted at the sight of her car pulling up front. She hated that as she left her house her head filled with the memory of that damned kiss.

Sliding into the passenger seat she gave him a bright smile and determined not to think about the kiss for the rest of the day. "Good morning," she said.

"Back at you," he replied and pulled away from the curb. "I heard from Trey this morning. Ray and Josh managed to find three eyewitnesses from last night. One said the car was black, another said it was blue and the third person was certain it was dark gray."

"Which basically means we'll probably never know who was behind the wheel," she replied. "I still think it was just some crazy nut speeding down the street who didn't see me. Maybe it was somebody texting while driving. I just don't believe that somebody intentionally tried to run me down. And now, what are the plans for today?"

"I'll let you know when we get to my place," he replied mysteriously.

"We still have a lot of people to talk to," she replied. "Even though we talked to Shelly's closest friends, she had lots of other friends in her life, and she might have confided something to a coworker at the Pirate's Inn."

Bo held a hand up, as if to stop her before she named every person in town. "We'll get there, Claire. How are you feeling? The knees doing okay?"

"The knees are already on the mend, although I have to confess that I'm feeling some aches in muscles I didn't know I had. What about you?"

"I feel a little beat up," he admitted. "We both had a hard landing last night." He pulled into his driveway, shut off the car and unbuckled his seat belt. "And that's why I've made the executive decision that we're taking the day off."

"The day off?" She looked at him blankly.

He offered her a small, sexy smile. "Yeah, you know, a day where we don't talk to anyone, we don't work the case and we just hang out and relax." He frowned suddenly. "Unless there's somebody else you'd rather hang out with for the day."

"No, not at all. I just assumed you'd be eager to push forward on the investigation."

"I am, but just not today." He got out of the car and Claire did the same and followed him into the house. Jimmy was sprawled in a recliner chair in the living room and he greeted her with his usual friendly smile. He grabbed the remote and muted the television, which was tuned to a news station.

"Heard you had an exciting evening last night," he said.

"Way too exciting for my taste," she replied and sat down on the sofa. She'd almost been nervous to spend the day in the house with Bo, afraid that he might try to kiss her again and she might let him. She'd forgotten that Jimmy would be here, too.

"Something to drink?" Bo asked, poised between the living room and kitchen.

As usual he was dressed in a pair of jeans and a dark gray T-shirt and looked hot and sexy. "Something cold, if it's not too much trouble," Claire said.

"Iced tea okay?"

She nodded her assent and he disappeared into the kitchen. "From what Bo tells me so far you haven't had much success in your investigation," Jimmy said.

"We've really only just started," she replied, refusing to be discouraged after a couple of days.

"I wish I could do something to help. Bo's like a brother to me. Without his friendship and support I probably would have become a no-account nasty drunk just like my father."

Claire smiled at him. "I had one of those, too. Although mine was a no-account absent father most of the time." Bo returned with two glasses of iced tea. He handed her one and then sat on the opposite side of the sofa and placed his glass on the coffee table in front of them.

"Bo told me that your mother left town when you were young. Have you ever heard from her?" Jimmy asked.

"No, and at this point in my life I have no desire to hear from her. She made her choice to cut and run and leave me behind and apparently never looked back. She wasn't there when I needed her and now I have no need of her. How's business?" she asked, ready to get the topic of conversation off herself and a childhood she couldn't change.

For the next few minutes Jimmy talked about the business that had once been Bo's. He entertained with stories of picky customers and crazy drunks, making both Claire and Bo laugh.

It felt good to laugh and to hear Bo's deep rumble of laughter. It felt good not to think about the investigation and everything she felt they still needed to do in order to accomplish their mission.

Bo was right. They'd needed a day off. He appeared more relaxed than she'd ever seen him. By one o'clock they had all moved into the kitchen for a late lunch. Jimmy insisted that she and Bo sit and leave the meal to him.

Within twenty minutes he served them hot ham and cheese sandwiches on toasted rye bread and French fries on the side. While they ate Jimmy continued to talk about the bar and grill and Claire found herself wondering if it bothered Bo that his best friend was now reaping the benefits of Bo's defection from town.

After lunch Bo and Jimmy entertained her with stories of their childhood antics. They had tales of sneaking out of the house at midnight to go frog gigging in the swamp and running home after only a few minutes, scared of the dark and the fear of being eaten by gators.

There were stories of building a tent in the backyard and then accidently setting it on fire when they decided to roast marshmallows inside the tent.

After each and every story they argued about who had been the one who had come up with the ideas that had usually gotten them into trouble as Claire laughed at the easy banter between the two friends.

"What about you, Claire? Do you have close girl-friends who do lunch with you or go out for drinks and gossip together?" Jimmy asked.

"I have lots of friendly acquaintances but no close girlfriends," she replied. She frowned thoughtfully, wondering why she had never encouraged any real solid friendships.

She knew that when she was young she'd never wanted anyone to know that she was basically living in a shanty that rarely had electricity on and no parental figure in the place.

"When I was young, I was afraid for anyone to find out that I was basically living alone. I was scared that social services would somehow find out and take me away," she continued. "I guess as I got older that self-protectiveness stuck with me and I just never formed close relationships."

"Then who do you talk to about your deepest, darkest secrets?" Bo asked.

She laughed. "I don't have any deep, dark secrets. What you see is what you get."

Bo's gaze lingered on her, his eyes silently seeming to tell her that he definitely liked what he saw. Warmth leaped into her cheeks and she was grateful when Jimmy began talking once again.

The rest of the afternoon passed pleasantly with the conversation remaining light and easy. About four o'clock Jimmy excused himself to get ready for his night of work, leaving Claire and Bo alone on the sofa.

"Isn't this better than being out in the heat and trying to talk to people who don't particularly want to talk to us?" Bo asked.

"It has been a nice break," she agreed. "But tomorrow I think I need to be boss again and we need to move forward in trying to find some answers."

"I only get to be boss for a day?" he asked in amusement.

"What you should want now more than anything is something that will lead us to Shelly's killer," she replied.

He leaned toward her, the scent of him filling her head and stirring up a tension that was both slightly frightening and exhilarating.

"You know what I want more than anything at this moment?" His blue eyes simmered as they held her gaze hypnotically. "I want a repeat of our kiss last night. In fact, I want more than that. I want you in my bed making love with me."

A soft gasp escaped her at the blatant sensuality of his gaze and the unfiltered words that filled her with an internal fire.

"Bo, we're partners, not lovers." She was appalled by the slightly breathless quiver in her voice.

"We could be both," he replied.

"I don't think that's a line we should cross." She knew her voice lacked conviction and she cursed herself for it.

"You're the boss," he replied and leaned back. "I just want you to know that if you change your mind, I'm open and interested."

Thankfully at that moment Jimmy returned to the living room and halted any further conversation on that subject. It was only when Jimmy left that she grew a bit nervous about how the rest of the evening would unfold.

She needn't have worried. Bo remained a perfect gentleman as they watched a movie together and then shared a pizza. Any talk of the investigation remained off-limits and instead they talked more about their pasts, talked about the changes that would occur in the town when the amusement park finally opened, and their favorite books and movies.

Before she knew it, dusk had fallen with night not too far behind. "I should head home," she said. "And we should figure out what our plans are for tomorrow. No more days off."

"But it has been nice, hasn't it? To spend the day together and not think about who said what, when, and not think about what neighbor or friend might be a cold-blooded killer," he replied.

"It has been nice," she agreed. "Maybe tomorrow we need to just talk to everyone we run into who was about the same age as Shelly. Maybe she had a close friend you didn't know about."

Bo heaved an exaggerated sigh. "Okay, boss. Why don't you pick me up around ten?"

"Sounds good." Claire got up from the sofa, grabbed her purse and headed for the door. Bo followed just behind her. When she reached the door she didn't turn to face him to say good-night. She knew instinctively he was too close behind her, that in turning to face him he might kiss her and she might kiss him back.

She opened the door and then the screen door and stepped out on his porch. Only then did she turn around and wave to him.

Once she was in her car and headed home she thought of last night when she'd told him she slept naked. What a stupid thing it had been for her to confess to a man who was obviously sexually attracted to her...a man she was sexually attracted to.

It was dark by the time she parked her car and went into the house. It was only when she set her purse on the table that she realized she hadn't retrieved her mail since Bo had shown up in town.

She opened her front door and headed for the mailbox near the street. The black of night surrounded her, broken only by a neighbor's porch light that shot a faint beam of illumination.

She reached the mailbox and was about to open it when she felt a sudden rush of air coming from behind her. Before she could turn, a plastic bag was yanked not only over her head, but down the length of her body to trap her arms against her sides, as well.

She screamed and kicked out with her legs. Disoriented and with her heart pounding in terror, her kicks didn't connect with anything or anyone. She tore at the plastic around her with her fingernails, attempting to free her arms.

Panicked screams continued to tear from her throat, rising in volume when she was picked up by strong arms.

It was only then that her brain made the connection that she was being kidnapped and there was nobody around to save her.

CLAIRE HAD BEEN gone for about forty-five minutes when Bo's cell phone rang. "It's Eric Baptiste," the caller's deep voice boomed over the line. "You need to get to Claire's." Without offering any more information, Eric hung up.

Bo stood staring at his phone, wondering if this was some sort of a setup? A prank of some sort? Eric didn't seem the type of man to pull a prank. His heart seemed to stop beating. Something had happened.

He grabbed his keys and within minutes was on his motorcycle speeding to Claire's house, his brain whirling with suppositions. Had she hurt herself? Fallen down and broken a bone? Then why would Eric call him instead of calling for an ambulance?

He didn't pay attention to the speed limit; he only knew he needed to get to Claire as quickly as possible. Why hadn't she called him? What could have possibly happened to her in the past forty-five minutes?

He pulled up in front of her place and parked. Jumping off his bike, he noticed a torn black trash bag in her yard. What the hell?

Not pausing, he raced to Claire's door. Eric answered the knock and the minute Bo stepped inside

Claire flew into his arms. Bo automatically wrapped his arms around her as she cried into his chest. What in the hell had happened?

He looked at Eric quizzically, but the well-built, dark-eyed man shrugged and sat in the chair opposite the sofa. Apparently it was Claire's story to tell.

At least physically she appeared to be fine, although obviously emotionally distraught. She had just begun to gain control and Bo had led her to the sofa where they sat down when a knock fell on the door and Sheriff Trey Walker and Deputy Ray McClure walked in, followed by Deputies Josh Griffin and Daniel Carson.

Trey looked at the three of them. "What happened?" He turned his attention to Eric. "You called about an attempted kidnapping?"

Bo's insides shuddered and he tightened his arm around Claire. "What happened?" he asked Claire, repeating Trey's words as Bo's blood iced in his veins.

"I left your house and when I got home I realized I hadn't checked my mail for a while." Her voice trembled and her face was paper white. "When I got to the mailbox I sensed somebody behind me but before I could turn around he pulled a garbage bag over me." Her eyes simmered with the terror she'd experienced. "I tried to fight, and I screamed over and over again, but he picked me up in his arms."

"Griffin and Carson, check out the area and see if anyone saw anything," Trey said.

"I was sitting on my porch and heard her screams,"

Eric said as the two men left the house. "I yelled and ran down here, but by that time whoever it was had dropped her to the ground and disappeared into the darkness."

"Eric ripped the bag off me and got me into the house and that's when he called Bo and you," she said to Trey.

"Did you get any idea of a description of the man?" Trey asked Eric.

Eric shook his head. "It was dark and he was dressed all in black. I only got a brief glimpse of him from the back."

"Short...tall...build?" Trey asked.

Eric shrugged helplessly. "It was just too dark for me to get any idea of size or shape. He was just a black form running away."

Trey focused back on Claire. "Did he say anything to you?"

"Nothing," she replied. "I can't tell you anything about him. I didn't see him. He didn't make a sound. I just know he was strong enough to pick me up like I weighed nothing."

Bo listened and even though she was safe and right next to him, his blood refused to warm. There was no way to dismiss this attack on Claire as anything but an intentional act.

This forced him to believe that the speeding car that had nearly hit her hadn't somehow been an attack on him, but on her.

"Can I go?" Eric asked. "I've told you everything I know."

Trey hesitated a moment and then nodded. "We'll be in touch if we have any more questions for you."

Eric left the chair and headed out the door and Trey sat in the newly vacated seat. Ray stood just behind him and spoke for the first time.

"Maybe it would be best if you two weren't spending so much time together," he said. "It's possible somebody is ticked off at you because you're trying to help Bo."

"Maybe it would be best if you'd do your job and find out who has tried to harm me twice now," she retorted, her fear momentarily displaced by a flash of anger.

"We're going to do everything we can to find this perp," Trey assured her with a calm that bordered on patronizing. "And you have every right to fraternize with anyone you want in this town."

"This certainly isn't going to stop me from spending time with Bo," she said and placed a hand on his thigh. It was then that Bo's blood began to warm again.

"Has anyone threatened you? Shown anger toward you?" Trey asked.

"No, nothing like that, although I did have a note taped to my porch railing a couple of nights ago that said 'stay away from Bo McBride.'"

Trey sat up straighter in the chair. "Do you still have the note?"

"No, I threw it away," Claire replied. She frowned. "I should have brought the note to you the minute I found it, but I just figured it was harmless, somebody trying to warn me not to get involved in Bo's issues."

Trey rubbed his forehead as if weary. "I have to look at this as if there have been two attacks on you and we don't have much to go on. We couldn't even get a confirmation on the color of the car that tried to hit you and now I have no description of the person who attacked you tonight."

"There is the garbage bag outside," Bo said.

Trey nodded. "We'll take it and see if we can pull some prints, but I'm not optimistic about it." He looked back at Ray. "Go outside and bag and tag the evidence." Ray immediately left to do his job.

Trey turned his attention back to Claire and Bo. "Is there anything else you can tell me?"

Bo looked at Claire, glad to see that some of the fear had left her eyes and her cheeks had once again filled with natural color. "I can't think of anything," she replied.

By that time Griffin and Carson had returned, indicating that they'd found no witnesses and no sign of the attacker.

Trey stood. "I intend to focus this investigation on people who are particularly upset with Bo. I think it's quite possible that your connection with him is the reason for these attacks. But if you think of anyone else who might have a reason to want to harm you for any reason, give me a call."

"Trust me, you'll be one of the first to know," Claire replied.

Once everyone was gone, Claire leaned against

Bo's side and released a tremulous sigh. She didn't speak, and in the silence Bo's thoughts flew as he tried to figure out what should happen now.

The idea that he was responsible for any threat to Claire was unacceptable. From the moment they'd started spending time together he'd never considered the possibility that he was putting her at risk.

"What a night," she finally said.

Bo tightened his arm around her. "I'm just glad you're okay." The idea of anything bad happening to her caused a huge lump to form in his chest, making it impossible for him to speak for a moment.

He'd already been through the agony of losing three people he loved: his father, his mother and Shelly. Although he wasn't in love with Claire, he cared about her deeply and refused to consider losing her to some nutcase with a grudge against him.

What had been the motive of the person who had attempted to take Claire tonight? Was it possible he'd simply meant to scare her, or had the person had deadly intentions? Was it possible the goal was to kill Claire and leave her body in the swampy lagoon in an effort to somehow frame Bo for another woman's murder? It would definitely shake everything up if Bo returned to town and another young woman was killed and left in the lagoon.

"Bo?"

Claire pulled him from his thoughts. "Sorry, I was just thinking about the next move for us," he replied.

She sat up straighter and he pulled his arm from around her. "What do you mean? The next move for us is that we keep doing what we're doing. We continue to try to find Shelly's killer."

"It's not that easy after what almost happened here tonight." He moved several inches away from her. "I have to consider that you having contact with me has put you in danger."

"If that's the case then I'm now on notice and can be better prepared," she replied with a lift of her chin. "I'm not going to let some creep dictate what I do and with whom."

Bo raked a hand through his hair, knowing that she was stubborn enough to continue the investigation with or without him, still putting her potentially at risk.

"As far as I'm concerned we have three options. The first is that I forget this whole thing and go back to Jackson. The second is that you forget this whole thing and distance yourself from me and anything to do with Shelly's murder."

"I don't like those options," she replied with a touch of petulance.

"The third option is that you move into my house where I can be sure that nobody can get to you again."

She stared at him, her eyes reflecting myriad emotions…apprehension, a touch of residual fear and something else he couldn't identify. "So you'd be like my personal bodyguard?"

"Exactly."

She frowned and looked around the room and

then back at him. "And it would be a strictly platonic roommate arrangement?"

"I would never take advantage of you, Claire," he replied softly.

"I have to admit, I'm more than a little shaken up by what happened, and the idea of being here all alone is a bit scary."

"Then pack a bag and let's get out of here," Bo replied.

As she disappeared into her bedroom, Bo quickly processed the bedroom situation at his place. His mother's bedroom still hadn't been completely cleared. The bed had been stripped and he wasn't sure he was emotionally ready to allow anyone to sleep in there yet.

The easiest thing to do was for Bo to put Claire in his bedroom, and he'd bunk on the sofa. There was a door that connected his room to his mother's bathroom and that would give Claire more privacy in a home where two men lived.

With the arrangements set in his head, he stood from the sofa and walked to the front window. He peered out into the darkness and wondered who in the hell had attacked Claire.

He'd known she wouldn't agree to stop investigating Shelly's murder. At this point he wasn't even sure she'd stop if he went back to Jackson. He was only grateful that she'd agreed to come to his place where he could make sure she stayed safe.

He turned away from the window as she came back into the living room, this time carrying a bulging duffel bag, a rigid set to her shoulders. "I hate that some creep is making me afraid to stay here," she said. "I hate being chased out of my own home."

"Hopefully, Trey and his men will get to the bottom of this quickly and before you know it you'll be back here."

She eyed him dubiously. "I don't have a lot of confidence in Trey and his men finding their way out of a paper bag. Trey is too busy sucking up to Mayor Jim Burns to be a good leader in the department. He doesn't want to solve crimes, he just wants any perks that come with his position."

She drew a deep breath. "Sorry, I'm rambling and being cranky."

"You're allowed to be cranky," he replied gently. "It's late and you've had a traumatic experience. Let's get out of here and get you settled in at my place."

Bo stepped out of the front door and onto the porch first and then froze. He was vaguely aware of Claire moving next to him even as his focus remained solely on the items on the porch.

"What the hell?" he muttered as Claire gasped.

On the porch was a beige doll that looked like a stuffed gingerbread man. Sexless and faceless, the doll sported three redheaded pins stabbed into the area that would be the doll's heart. There was also a note written in bold red lettering big enough to read by the living room light Claire had left on, which flowed through the front window.

YOU BELONG TO ME!!!!! The words screamed from the page and once again Bo's blood chilled.

Chapter Eight

It was just after two and Claire was snuggled beneath sheets that smelled of Bo. She'd been too upset to argue with him even when she'd realized that in giving her his room, he planned on sleeping on the sofa.

All she'd really been able to think about was that her harmless secret admirer was obviously an obsessed stalker who no longer wanted to date her but wanted to kill her.

They hadn't touched the voodoo doll or note but rather had called Trey back to the house where he'd collected the evidence. Then they had followed him to the station where she'd told him about the notes and flowers she'd received from somebody she hadn't given a minute's thought to in the past week or two.

Trey had questioned her for about an hour, forcing her to think about each note she'd received, the kind of vases that had been left and who she thought might be her secret admirer.

She'd had little information to give him. She'd been in a state of shock after realizing the threats against her weren't because of her helping Bo prove his innocence, but rather specifically directed at her and had nothing to do with Bo. She'd gotten her first notes and letters long before Bo had shown up in Lost Lagoon.

She now shivered and pulled the sheet up closer around her neck despite the warmth of the room. Her breathing grew shallow as she remembered those moments of being trapped in the plastic bag, unable to see her assailant and incapable of fighting back.

What would have happened if Eric hadn't been sitting on his front porch, if he hadn't heard her scream? She believed she'd be dead.

What had changed her secret admirer from a person who left her sweet little notes and freshly bloomed flowers to a madman who had tried to run her over with a car and kidnap her?

Ultimately she thought maybe it did come back to Bo. Whoever was after her was jealous and angry that she and Bo had been spending every waking hour together. The creep probably thought she and Bo were lovers and in his warped mind she'd belonged to him and now deserved to die for cheating on him.

She'd seen television shows and documentaries about stalking and obsessive love. The cases didn't always end well. She shivered again, and fear once again rose up inside her. She'd been damned for something that hadn't even happened. Her stalker felt she'd betrayed him with Bo. *But you could make it happen*, a little voice whispered inside her head. *You could make it happen right now.*

She thought of being held in Bo's arms, of his lips taking hers as their bodies melded together. Partners with benefits, he'd joked. But tonight was no joke. She wanted him. She needed him to take her away from her own scary thoughts.

Why not make love with Bo? She knew he wasn't her happily-ever-after, but at the moment that's not what she needed from him. She needed his warmth, his heart beating next to hers. She wanted him to assure her that she'd truly survived the night and that her life wasn't just about fear.

Without giving herself a chance to rethink her desire, she got out of bed and pulled her robe around her. If he was already asleep, then she wouldn't wake him.

She crept down the darkened hallway and paused at the threshold into the living room. "Bo?" she whispered.

By the moonlight drifting through the living room windows she saw him sit straight up. "Claire, is something wrong?"

"I've decided I want to be partners with benefits and I want to explore those benefits right now." Speaking the words out loud only made her more certain that she wanted him.

The physical attraction, the sexual tension between them, was undeniable, and they were both single, consenting adults. She was no starry-eyed romantic who expected anything from him other than the physical pleasure and sense of safety she knew she'd find in his arms tonight.

"Claire, you've had a traumatic night." He didn't move from the sofa. "Maybe now isn't the time to make a decision you'll later regret."

"I don't believe in living with regret," she replied. "Trust me, I know what I'm doing. I want you to make love to me, even if it's just for this one night." She gripped her thin cotton robe closer around her, wondering if she was making a complete fool of herself.

He stood. Clad only in a pair of black boxers and with the moonlight appearing to be drawn as if by magic to shimmer on every muscle and lean structure on his body, Claire's breathing grew shallow once again, only this time it had nothing to do with fear.

She nearly stopped breathing as he advanced toward her. He stopped when he stood inches from her, his body warmth radiating out to engulf her; his mere closeness drove every bad thought and fear out of her head.

"Claire." He raised a hand and placed it on her cheek. "You know I want you, but I also need you to know that I'm not looking for a relationship."

"Neither am I. I'm just looking for tonight." She turned her face into his palm and kissed it. "Just tonight, Bo."

He moved his hand from her face to the back of her head and pulled her against him as his mouth found hers. He tasted of fiery desire and mindless pleasure, exactly what she'd wanted, what she needed from him.

When the kiss finally ended, her knees were almost too weak to lead him down the hallway to his bedroom. The room was completely dark with only a faint sliver of moonlight whispering through the crack in the blinds.

Claire shrugged out of her robe and immediately got into the bed and covered up with the sheet. Bo took a moment longer and she knew he was taking off his boxers.

When he got beneath the covers with her there was nothing between them. They were warm skin and hard muscles and soft curves as he pulled her into his arms and their lips once again found each other.

As he kissed her, his arms moved from around her and his hands began to explore her. He caressed her shoulders, and then glided his palms across her breasts. Her nipples hardened at the brief touch as his hands continued a path down the flat of her stomach and then down the sides of her hips.

It was as if he were a blind man seeking to "see" her through his fingertips. It was also an erotic dance of touch that left her shivering with a desire she'd never felt before.

She reciprocated, running her fingers across his broad shoulders and chest. His stomach was an easy six-pack of taut muscles and before she could caress him any further he rolled over on top of her, his hardness against her as he kissed and tongued first one breast and then the other.

She tangled her hands in his hair, her hips automatically moving beneath him as the fire inside her grew to mammoth proportions.

She felt as if from the moment she'd met him they'd indulged in some form of foreplay that had her ready for him to take her now, this instant.

But he seemed to be in no hurry as he stroked her skin and kissed her lips, her throat, and once again covered one of her breasts with his mouth. A gasp escaped her as he licked and teased the taut pebble. She squeezed his shoulder muscles, mindless with pleasure. He was fire and she was being consumed by his flames.

Wanting to bring him as much pleasure, she reached between them and grasped his hardness. He hissed a swift intake of breath at her intimate touch.

She stroked him slowly, loving the feel of his velvet-soft skin encasing rock-hard and ready muscle. And then he touched her intimately, moving his fingers against her most sensitive spot.

She tried to maintain her focus on pleasuring him, but as his fingers moved more quickly her intentions disappeared beneath the building tide of imminent combustion.

Her climax shuddered through her, first tightening every muscle in her body and then leaving her weak, gasping and boneless.

Before she could catch her breath he positioned himself between her thighs and entered her. She closed her eyes and reveled in the fact that his body surrounded her and filled her.

He whispered her name just before he captured

her lips with his, kissing her with fervency, with passion unleashed. His hips moved against hers and she wrapped her legs around his back to pull him closer, deeper into her.

He stroked faster, finding a rhythm that once again built up a tension inside her that was both tormenting and exhilarating.

Once again he took her over the edge and at the same time she heard him gasp her name as he stiffened against her in his own release.

She unwound her legs from around him and he rolled to his back next to her. The only sound was of them both trying to catch their breath. Although she couldn't see him in the darkness of the room, she felt his movement against the mattress and knew he'd shifted positions. She turned on her side in his direction.

"That was amazing and totally irresponsible." His breath was warm on her face.

She knew immediately what he was talking about. "I'm not promiscuous, and I'm on the pill," she replied.

"Then I'll just go back to the fact that it was amazing," he replied. "And I haven't been with anyone since Shelly."

Claire was surprised and touched by the admission, somehow honored that she'd been the first woman since his lost love. "Thank you, Bo."

He laughed. "Don't thank me for doing something I wanted to do and would do again anytime of the day or night."

Once again she felt the mattress move and saw the faint illumination of him standing next to the bed. "Get some sleep, Claire. It will soon be morning."

Although she was disappointed that he apparently had no intention of staying with her for the rest of the night, the fear that had chilled her before they'd made love was gone, banished by what they'd just shared and the knowledge that she was safe in his home.

"Good night, Bo," she said, already drowsy as the last of her adrenaline seeped away.

"I'll see you in the morning," he said and then he was gone.

Claire curled up on her side and hugged the pillow where his head had just lain to her chest. She definitely wasn't eager to face the morning when she'd have to fully embrace the frightening thought that somebody close to her, somebody who had been her "secret admirer," no longer wanted to date her, but potentially had murder on his mind.

Chapter Nine

Despite the late night, Bo was awake at seven. He remained half tangled in the sheet that covered him as he thought about the events of the night before.

There was no question in his mind that Claire's secret admirer had gone rabid and was now a real and present threat to her safety.

Thinking about what had occurred between them in the darkness of night sent a surge of warmth through him. Making love with her had been everything he'd imagined and more. The scent of her, the taste of her, was now in his blood, and having her once wasn't enough.

But he knew if they made love again it would only be at her bidding. She was in control of that aspect of their "partnership." He had nothing more to offer her than the here and now, and the last thing he wanted was for emotions to get tangled up and messy and lead to heartbreak for either one of them.

There was no question that he cared about her a lot, but that didn't mean he was willing to ever give his heart to any woman or to Lost Lagoon again.

Claire had a good life here. She loved her work and the people, and she would continue to have a good life here long after he was gone. But first they had to figure out who had tried to take her last night; who possessed a twisted love for Claire that had turned into something dangerous?

Thoughts of her safety pulled him up from the sofa and down the hall to the bathroom. Thankfully before he'd turned his bedroom over to Claire the night before he'd grabbed clean clothes for today.

It took him only minutes to shower, dress and then head into the kitchen to get the coffee brewing. Jimmy wouldn't be up for hours and he hoped that Claire slept in, as well.

While waiting for the coffee, he dug around in one of the drawers at the small desk in the corner of the kitchen and found a new notebook. He carried it and a pen to the table and set it in the center.

Starting today they would not be working from Claire's notebook on Shelly's death. They would begin a brand-new investigation to find the identity of her secret admirer.

He finally sat at the table and curled his fingers around a mug of the fresh brew and thought about their second interaction with Trey the night before.

The lawman had appeared to take everything seriously, including the fact that the perp had obviously been watching Claire's house while they'd been there the first time that night.

The doll and note hadn't been on the porch when Bo had initially arrived, nor had they been there when Trey and his men had first shown up. Whoever had placed the items on the porch had waited until the lawmen had left, indicating that he'd been watching the place the whole time.

The only name Claire had mentioned to Trey in the way of suspects was Neil Sampson, the city councilman she'd dated and broken up with months before.

Bo intended to press her this morning to come up with some other potential suspects. Claire was bright and beautiful and he couldn't imagine fewer than several men being attracted to her. She might be too obtuse or too naive to recognize their friendly smiles as some sort of sick romantic interest.

It was just after nine and Bo was sipping on his third cup of coffee when Claire appeared in the kitchen. She wore a pair of denim shorts and a red T-shirt and brought with her the scent of minty soap and fruity shampoo.

"Sleep well?" he asked and watched her beeline to the coffee.

"Surprisingly well, considering everything." She poured herself a cup of coffee and then joined him at the table. She nodded toward the notebook. "What's that?"

"You said you like notebooks, so that's the one for our new investigation. From here on out I'll be the boss of this operation and the investigation into who killed Shelly has once again become a cold case. We need to focus on your secret admirer."

She held up a hand. "Let me have a couple drinks

of coffee and process the shock of you being in charge before we talk about anything else."

Bo grinned, finding her charming. He was grateful that she obviously had no intention of talking about what had happened between them the night before.

She took two sips of her coffee and then set her cup back on the table. "If I don't get to be boss, then can I still be the official note-taker?"

"Absolutely," he replied and reached out to pull the notebook closer to her. "You told Trey last night that the only person you could think of in your life who could potentially be your secret admirer was Neil Sampson."

"He was the only person I could think of, and actually I can't imagine Neil being my admirer. The anonymous notes and flower thing just isn't his style."

"Maybe he stepped out of his comfort zone to get cutesy in an effort to win you back," Bo relied. He motioned toward the notebook. "His name should go on our suspect list."

She reached across the table to grab the pen and then opened up the notebook to the first page. In neat lettering she wrote "Suspects" across the top of the page and then placed Neil's name on the first line.

"What about your coach friend, Roger?" Bo asked.

She shook her head. "Roger is a good friend and coworker, but he has the hots for Mary Armstrong who works at the diner. He has no romantic interest in me."

"Write his name down anyway," Bo said. "Right now we need to view any man who has any interaction with you as a potential suspect."

She took another sip of her coffee and then wrote down Roger's name. "I hate this. I hate to think of one of my friends being a nutcase who wants to kill me."

Bo knew exactly how she felt. He'd felt the same emotion in the months following Shelly's death. He'd hated that he'd looked at everyone with suspicion, that an innocence he hadn't even known he possessed had been shattered and had never been regained.

He took a drink of his coffee, knowing the next name he was going to throw out would shock her. But he'd played and replayed what she'd told Trey had happened the night before and he still had so many questions that he knew she couldn't answer.

"I think you need to add Eric Baptiste," he said and watched her beautiful blue eyes widen and then narrow in disbelief.

"Why would I put him on the list? He's been like a big brother to me. He saved me last night."

"Did he?" Bo countered. "Did you hear him yell at your attacker like he told Trey he did? Did you hear the sound of your attacker running away?"

She slowly shook her head. "I couldn't hear anything in that plastic bag except the terrified beating of my heart and my own screams." She wrapped her slender fingers around her cup, as if seeking warmth as she gazed at him curiously. "Exactly what are you implying?"

"I'm just wondering if maybe Eric was the person who attacked you and then saved you."

"And why on earth would he do something so crazy?"

"To be your hero," Bo replied. "If he's your secret admirer then he obviously has or had a romantic interest in you. He sees you spending all your time with me and he gets worried that we have something romantic going on so he sets up a scenario where he can save you from the bad guy and you'll see him as a hero, and every woman loves a hero."

She stared at him as if he'd dropped to the table from another planet. "I should be worried that you could actually come up with that take on the situation."

"I've had a lot of time and a lot of coffee to fuel all kinds of thoughts. I even wondered about Mac Sinclair potentially being your secret admirer."

"But he's married," she protested.

Bo raised a dark eyebrow. "That doesn't always stop a man from wanting a little on the side. I know that sounds crass, but the fact is some men cheat."

Claire leaned back in her chair and frowned thoughtfully. "If Mac was leaving me love notes and flowers, then he'd be particularly enraged by me hooking up with you, the man he thinks killed his sister."

"You need to write down both of their names and

then we need to call Trey to let him know that you've thought of more people who might guilty."

"There's one thing I'd like to do today," she replied. "I want to stop in at Mama Baptiste's shop. If I remember right the doll last night was from a kit that she sells to tourists in her shop."

"A kit?"

She nodded. "It comes with a couple of markers, some yarn to make hair and the pins to stick into the doll. They're a silly, harmless nod to voodoo that appeal to people who don't live in the South and think voodoo is still alive and well in all the Southern Gulf states."

"She should be selling pirate stuff since the legend of the town is that pirates once used the area as their stronghold."

"Trust me, she has plenty of pirate items to sell, too. Of course her real business is her herbal skills, and there are people in town who depend on her homeopathic remedies."

"I imagine Trey will be investigating where the doll came from and will talk to her."

"I'd still like to talk to her myself. Besides, it's been a while since I've seen her."

"Okay," Bo agreed. "We'll eat breakfast and then go to her shop."

It was an hour later that they left the house in Claire's car and headed to Mama Baptiste's shop on Main Street. They'd called Trey to give him the list of names they'd come up with over coffee and Trey had vowed to check each man's alibi for the night before.

A bell tinkled as they walked into the small shop, which held enough items that it could have used three times the space. The front of the store had shelves and wall displays with a variety of tourist-type items.

Overhead and throughout the entire store, herbs and roots hung over exposed wooden rafters, apparently used in the magical concoctions Mama Baptiste brewed up for her customers.

She stood behind a counter in the center of the store and Claire made a beeline for the woman who had helped her get through her difficult childhood.

Mama Baptiste was a tall plump woman with long black hair shot through with shiny silver strands. She was clad in a bright yellow peasant-style blouse and a long multicolored skirt that gave her a gypsy aura.

She stepped out from around the counter and greeted Claire with a big, long hug. "I heard what happened last night," she said as she finally released Claire. "Thank goodness you're okay."

"I'm fine," Claire replied.

Mama Baptiste's dark eyes turned to focus on Bo. "Only a foolish or an innocent man would come back here and stir up old wounds. Which are you, Bo McBride?"

Her gaze was so intense it was as if she were looking right into the center of his heart, his very soul. He felt as though he were strapped to a lie detector machine. "Innocent," he replied without hesitation.

She held his gaze for another long moment and then nodded, seeming satisfied. She looked back at

Claire. "You rarely come to my shop so I'm assuming this isn't a social stop."

"Actually, I'm here about the voodoo doll kits you sell," Claire replied.

Mama Baptiste motioned toward a wall display toward the front of the store. "There are the kits, but I can't tell you the last time I sold one. As you know, we don't get many tourists coming through town."

Bo followed Claire to the display and immediately recognized the dolls in the kits as the same kind that had been left on Claire's porch the night before.

He turned back to Mama. "Is there any other place in town that sells these?"

"Not that I know of," she replied. "There aren't many places in town that sell tourist items, although I'm sure that will change once the amusement park is up and running and we actually have tourists wandering in and out of the stores."

"You said you don't remember the last time you sold one of the dolls. Do you keep records that you could look at or keep an inventory list that would tell you if perhaps one was stolen?" Bo asked.

"Bookkeeping isn't my strong suit. I don't keep those kind of records except for my apothecary business." She looked at him apologetically. "Unfortunately, I can't help you with the doll."

Bo was disappointed, but he also knew how easy it would be for Eric to take one of the dolls without his mother ever knowing. For that matter, they hung close enough to the door of the shop that anyone could steal one.

Mama Baptiste and Claire visited for a few more minutes and then left, nearly bumping into Mac Sinclair, who was about to enter the shop.

Mac was shorter than Bo, with the Sinclair dark hair and brown eyes... Eyes that narrowed ominously at the same time his hands balled into fists at his side.

"Well, if it isn't the town's newest happy couple," he said with a half sneer as his gaze locked with Bo's. "Come back to town to find another beautiful, innocent woman you can use and then throw away in the lagoon?"

Bo remained silent, refusing to be baited. Mac turned his gaze to Claire and instantly his features softened. "Claire, what are you doing with this scum? Don't you know that there are people who would be happy to see him dead? I'd hate to see you get caught up in any cross fire if and when bad things happen."

He didn't wait for a reply, but shoved past them and into the shop. Bo stared after him and for the first time in his life he wished he had a gun, because he felt that danger was inching closer with every minute that passed.

"WAS THAT A direct threat?" Claire asked as they got back into her car.

"I don't know if it was a threat or a warning," Bo replied. "I wonder how his marriage is going?"

"What does that have to do with anything?" she asked.

"Mac said you were beautiful and there was a

tenderness in his eyes when he looked at you. You've never had any interaction with him?"

"Just the casual kind. He stopped into George's burger joint about once a week and we'd visit but nothing about him ever gave me the heebie-jeebies." She definitely had the heebie-jeebies now, not just about Mac but about every man in town. Who was after her? Who wanted her dead?

"What do you want to do now?" he asked.

She looked at him with a small smile. "I thought you were boss of this operation."

"I am, but I'm open to suggestions."

"Let's go get an ice cream cone," she said impulsively. "It's not quite as hot today and we can sit at one of the umbrella tables outside and people-watch."

"Is this part of a master plan to identify your admirer or an avoidance of the issue altogether?"

"Maybe a little bit of both," she admitted. She'd love to be able to forget that somebody had an unhealthy obsession with her. She'd love to pretend that she and Bo were partners not just in crime, but also in love.

She froze as she realized the dangerous path her thoughts had taken her. She was falling in love with Bo despite all of her wishes to the contrary. Making love with him last night had not only been a physical need, it had been an emotional one, as well.

She'd just been fooling herself into believing she was in complete control of her emotions where he was concerned. With his gentle kisses to her boo-boos, with that slow, sexy grin of his that heated her through and through and the quick wit that either kept her questioning things or laughing, he'd sneaked beneath her defenses.

"Earth to Claire." His deep voice broke through her thoughts and she realized they had parked in front of the ice cream parlor. "You disappeared on me for a moment there." He shut off the car engine.

"I was just trying to decide what kind of ice cream sounded good," she said with a forced lightness.

Minutes later they sat at one of the small color-ful umbrella tables on a small patio just outside the parlor. Claire held a chocolate mint ice cream cone while Bo had opted for a peanut butter blend.

As he licked his cone she tried not to think about how his tongue had felt against her skin the night be-fore. Dammit, she was supposed to be thinking about the possible identity of her attacker and instead she couldn't help herself from thinking about a one-night stand with a man who was certain to break her heart.

She looked out at the sidewalk and sat up straighter in her chair as she saw Roger walking to-ward them, a wide grin on his face.

"Claire…Bo," he greeted them. "Mind if I join you for a moment?"

"Pull up a chair," Bo replied.

Roger grabbed a chair from another table and pulled it up to theirs and sat. "Claire, I stopped by your house earlier to see if you wanted to meet me at the gym and get in a little workout."

She licked the quickly melting ice cream cone

and then replied, "This is the only workout I have in mind for the day."

Roger leaned forward slightly. "I also wanted to tell you that I did it. I asked Mary out."

"Roger, that's great!" She held her hand up for a high five. "When and where?"

"Day after tomorrow," he replied. "She's off that night and I promised her I'd take her someplace where she would be served rather than her doing the serving."

"Not many fine restaurants to pick from in this town," Bo said.

"We decided to do casual at the pizza place. That's good for a first date, isn't it?" He looked at Claire with a touch of concern.

"It's a perfect choice for a first date," Claire assured him.

Roger appeared relieved. He jumped up out of his chair. "Well, I'll just leave you two to enjoy the rest of the afternoon." He moved his chair back to the table where it belonged and carefully aligned it in place, then waved to them and headed on down the sidewalk.

"There's no way he should be on my list of suspects," she said and then popped the last of the cone into her mouth. It was as if that last bite held more than a little bit of discouragement.

She'd been excited to help Bo clear his name and identify a killer, but she wasn't so eager to do anything to try to find her stalker. She couldn't believe that anyone she had written down on her list of potential suspects was guilty, and she didn't know where else to look for a creep.

"What next?" Bo asked as they got back into her car.

"To be honest, I think I'd just like to go back to your place. I think maybe I need some more down-time to process everything that has happened."

"Whatever you need, Claire," he replied gently and it didn't take long for them to be back at his house.

Jimmy was up and in a chair with the television tuned to a talk show. "Did you solve all the mysteries already?"

"No, we just decided to take the rest of the day off," Bo replied.

"Let Trey and his men do the work," Claire said and sank onto the sofa. She felt oddly vulnerable, with the horror of the near-kidnapping the night before and the realization that she was more than half in love with Bo weighing heavily on her mind.

"In fact, if nobody minds I think I'm going to take a nap," she continued. After the short night maybe a nap was just what she needed to get herself into a better frame of mind.

"Are you okay?" Bo asked in obvious concern.

She got up from the sofa. "I'm fine. I'm overtired and maybe a little overwhelmed by everything. A nap will set me right." She offered Bo a reassuring smile and then headed for the bedroom.

Once there she kicked off her shoes and curled

up in the center of the neatly made bed. She closed her eyes but her mind refused to quiet.

Her thoughts didn't race to make sense of her feelings for Bo, but rather what her attacker had intended for her the night before.

The pins in the heart of the voodoo doll definitely indicated somebody who wanted her dead, but why hadn't the attacker simply stabbed her in the yard or shot her as she'd made her way to her mailbox?

The assailant hadn't wanted her dead by her mailbox. His intention had been to carry her off somewhere. And do what with her? Kill her at another location? Chain her up in some cellar or isolated place where he could rape and beat her before finally killing her?

The note she'd received warning her to stay away from Bo McBride she now believed was a warning from her secret admirer and not some note from a concerned friend or neighbor. And that note and her continuing relationship with Bo had transformed obsessed love into mad rage for somebody.

Who? Who had killed Shelly Sinclair two years ago and who wanted Claire dead now? She finally drifted off to sleep and dreamed of being held in a dark, dank cellar with no hope for rescue.

They stayed in Bo's house for the next two days, their only information about the attack on her coming from Trey. There had been no fingerprints found on the doll, the note or the garbage bag.

He'd checked the alibis of the men on the list Claire had provided with a variety of results. Mac

Sinclair had been at home with his wife. Roger had been home alone, as had Neil Sampson. Eric, of course, had been at the scene.

Basically the investigation was going nowhere, but in the two days she and Bo had spent together their relationship had deepened as their close proximity had been conducive to heart-to-heart talks about their past and present.

She'd also learned when they'd played several games of chess that he was as competitive as she was, that his laughter was often contagious and that he had the ability to make her feel like she was the most special woman on the face of the planet.

If she'd been on the verge of being in love with Bo before, the two days had only intensified her love for him. She had no idea what he felt toward her. It was obvious he was physically attracted to her and that he cared about her well-being.

In any case, it didn't matter what he felt for her, as their time together would eventually end and she'd return to her life with only heart scars to show that he'd once been here.

That was if the person tormenting her was caught, when that person was no longer a danger. She couldn't stay with Bo forever and could only hope that Trey and his men found the guilty party so that she could gain some needed distance from Bo.

Each night when she got into bed, she thought about calling to him to join her again, to make love to her once more, but in the end she denied herself the pleasure, knowing that it would only make things harder on her when it came time for him to say goodbye.

She didn't want to leave the safety of his house and yet felt a restless need to escape the confines. She was accustomed to being out and about town during the days, enjoying the leisure of summer before school began again in the fall.

She was particularly restless when she went to bed on the third night of being cooped up. She'd never considered herself a coward before, but her desire to stay inside was definitely built on the roots of fear and the perverse desire for her admirer not to be able to see her, to get close to her in any way.

Although the mattress was comfortable and the last couple of nights' sleep had found her easily, tonight she stared up at the ceiling as slumber refused to come.

There was little moonlight tonight and finally at eleven thirty, still unable to sleep, she got out of bed and moved the curtains aside to peer into the dark night.

Adrenaline filled her and she suddenly knew exactly what she wanted to do.

Chapter Ten

"Bo?"

He sat straight up at the sound of Claire calling his name. Immediately his thoughts went to holding her in his arms, making love to her again. That was almost all he'd been able to think about over the past three days.

"Yeah?" His voice was deeper than usual, husky even to his own ears.

"Get dressed."

He frowned at her unexpected words. "Get dressed? Why?"

"It's a perfect night for ghost hunting," she replied. "I'll be back in just a few minutes." He heard her soft footfalls returning to his bedroom.

He raked a hand through his hair and then reached in the darkness for the jeans at the foot of the sofa. He'd hoped she'd call to him again, wanting... needing him, but certainly not for a night of ghost hunting.

Once he had his jeans pulled up, he turned on the living room light. He pulled on the white T-shirt he'd had on before going to bed and then sat on the sofa to wait for Claire.

This wasn't exactly what he'd had in mind for a Friday night. If he was going to be awakened by her, he'd hoped for something far different.

She appeared in the living room dressed in a pair of denim jean shorts and a peach-colored sleeveless blouse that buttoned up the front. Her blue eyes simmered with an excitement he hadn't seen over the past couple of days.

"Are you dragging me out of the house in the middle of the night on a wild-goose chase?" he asked.

"Probably," she replied with a cheeky grin. "But from the rumors I've heard, tonight seems like the perfect night to catch a sight of Shelly's ghost walking around the edge of the lagoon."

Bo couldn't help a snort of disbelief. "I don't believe in ghosts," he replied.

"Then you don't want to go?" she asked, obviously crestfallen.

"Nah, I'll go. I'll indulge you in your craziness. If nothing else we'll get out of the house for a little while." He was rewarded with one of her beatific smiles that made him feel bigger, stronger and better than he was. Those smiles of hers could become addictive to him if he allowed it.

"We need to walk," she said. "The sound of any vehicle might scare the ghost off."

"I'll grab a flashlight." He left the living room and went into the kitchen, where he not only grabbed a flashlight from the cabinet beneath the sink but also opened one of the desk drawers and pulled out a pocketknife with a wicked blade.

He'd bought the knife off another kid at school when he was fifteen, then had made the mistake of showing it off to his mother. She'd immediately taken the knife from him and had grounded him for a week.

He'd forgotten about the weapon until the day before, when he'd been digging in the drawer to find a paper clip that Claire had wanted for her notebook.

He slipped the knife into his back pocket. There was no way he wanted to be out in the dark with Claire and not have some form of protection. He'd certainly prefer a gun, but the knife would have to do. Besides, he didn't really expect any trouble.

"We have about fifteen minutes to get to the bushes in front of the edge of the lagoon," she said when he returned to the living room. "Supposedly the ghost always walks around midnight."

"Of course she does," he said drily. "At what other time would a ghost walk the night?" He locked the door and they were on their way, the humid night air wrapping around them. "Does she also rattle chains as she walks?"

His sarcastic comment was met with an elbow to his rib. "Laugh now, Mr. Nonbeliever, at least I have an open mind."

The street was dark between the lamps that marked each block and Bo grabbed Claire's hand, not quite trusting what might be lurking in that darkness. They'd already been ambushed twice; he didn't want to be caught unaware again.

They left Bo's street and crossed to another, moving in the direction of the tip of the lagoon and the swampy area that surrounded it.

The night felt ominous, with wisps of low-lying fog appearing as they got closer to the swamp. The houses they passed were dark, the residents asleep in their beds as most sane people should be. A dog barked, breaking the silence.

Claire moved closer to him and he squeezed her hand, wondering what in the hell they'd been thinking of when they'd decided to leave the house in the middle of the night.

"You know I'm probably the only man on the face of the earth who would indulge you in this craziness," he murmured softly.

"I know," she replied and this time she squeezed his hand tight.

When they drew closer to the swamp, the air smelled of fish and rotten vegetation, a scent that Bo knew was familiar to them both. On stagnant, hot summer days the smell of the swamp permeated the whole town.

The silence of the night also filled with noise as they got nearer to the swamp. Bullfrogs croaked, and splashes created by fish jumping or gators slapping their tails could be heard.

A knot of tension balled up in Bo's stomach. He knew just ahead of them was the stone bench where he and Shelly had met on so many nights. Just behind

the bench a long row of bushes created a barrier between safe land and the lagoon ten feet beyond. It
was in those bushes that Shelly had struggled with
somebody to her death.

While he would always grieve the loss of her as a
beautiful woman he'd once loved, he'd also come to
the realization that they would have never married.

At the time of her death Shelly had one foot with
him in Lost Lagoon and her other foot pointed in
the direction of a bigger, more exciting future someplace else.

Had there been another man involved? Had that
been the sticky situation that had troubled her before her death? And had she fought with that man
that fatal night?

If she'd lived, Bo knew that the vision she had
of a life outside of Lost Lagoon would have won in
the end. Still, knowing that didn't make being at the
place of her murder any easier.

He would have rather lost her to another man than
to death. Yes, she'd been his first love, and he'd made
the decision when she was gone that she would be
his last love.

They approached the bushes on the left side of
the bench and heard some giggling coming from the
bushes to the right side. Bo shone his flashlight in
the faces of three teenage girls who were crouched
down.

"Shut off that light," one of them said. "You'll
scare away the ghost." Her admonishment was followed by a new round of excited giggling.

Bo turned off the flashlight and crouched down beside Claire. "We've got to be out of our minds," he whispered. She grabbed his hand once again.

"At least we're a little bit crazy together," she whispered back.

The moonlight spilled but a mere sliver of illumination and the low-lying fog was thicker here, making it impossible for him to see Claire's features. She was only a dark form next to him, a woman he would know in any depth of darkness by her heady scent and by the familiar heat of her body so close to his.

Part of him wanted to leave town now, to climb on his bike and finally put Lost Lagoon behind him forever. Claire was getting too deep inside his heart, and he wouldn't allow love into his heart again.

He no longer cared about clearing his name. The odds of them finding out the real killer after two years and without law enforcement's help were minimal at best.

However, the danger to Claire was real and present, and he couldn't leave town until he knew she was no longer at risk. Shelly and her murder would always be a piece of his past that would haunt him, but as soon as this issue with Claire was resolved it was time for him to leave and get on with his life in Jackson.

It was ironic that Shelly had wanted to leave Lost Lagoon and Bo had wanted to stay in the small town where his mother lived and his business thrived. With Claire it was the opposite: she loved her life here in Lost Lagoon and had probably never considered moving away from the job she loved and the people she'd always known all of her life.

It was a lose-lose situation for them that only confirmed to him that he was a man meant to live his life alone. Besides, he wasn't in love with Claire, he told himself firmly. He just cared about her and her safety and suffered a healthy dose of lust where she was concerned.

She was the first person in town who had been kind to him. She was one of the few people who believed in his innocence. She was bright and funny and sexy as hell. It was no great mystery that he was drawn to her.

He heard the teenagers begin to squeal. He and Claire raised their heads above the brush and Bo gasped as he saw a figure appear at the right of the grassy area between the bench, the bushes and the swamp.

It was a human figure, clad all in white from shoulders to toes and with long dark hair just like Shelly's. She appeared to be lit from within as she glided gracefully across the area and toward the opposite side of the space.

"Shelly! It's Shelly!" The teenagers squealed in a combination of excitement and terror. "It's her ghost."

It certainly looked like the ghost of Shelly, but Bo noticed that the woman never turned her face toward them and he caught a glimpse of black sneakers on her feet.

Since when did ghosts wear sneakers? He grabbed

his flashlight and leaped over the brush at the same time the "ghost" reached the other side of the open area and disappeared into the overgrown brush near the swamp's edge.

There was no place for her to go without walking back out. He assumed that whenever she made her walks she waited until anyone who had watched the spectacle went home and then left the cover of the wooded area.

She wouldn't have that same luxury tonight. He took the same route she took and crashed through the woods, his flashlight scanning the area for any sign of her.

She'd be trapped between the swamp and a high rise of land that was impossible to climb. It was a relatively small area to search and Bo wanted to know who was playing such a sick game for the entertainment of giggling school girls.

He shone his flashlight from side to side, expecting to see a white-clad teenager who was pretending to play the role of the ghost of a dead young woman. Instead he found nothing. Nobody crouched beneath thick brush, nobody hidden behind a tree…nothing.

There was no way out and yet she was gone… seemingly vanished into thin air just like a ghost.

"I'm telling you that was no ghost," Bo said to Claire as they began the walk home. "That was a real person pretending to be a ghost."

"Then how do you explain the fact that you didn't catch her? That she totally disappeared?" Claire asked.

"I can't," he said, his frustration obvious in his voice. "But somebody is playing a sick game and I don't like it. I'd love to find out who it is and why she's doing it."

"Yet another mystery to add to the growing list," Claire replied. She hadn't been fooled into believing the "apparition" had been the ghost of Shelly. What she couldn't imagine was why somebody would do such a thing. What was there to gain by pretending to be Shelly, dead and walking at the place of her murder?

She and Bo strolled at a leisurely pace as they started the trip back to his house. "There is a person who got away with murder, a crazy stalker after me and now somebody impersonating a dead woman. The whole world seems to have gone crazy," she said.

"Number one on my priority list is making sure you stay safe and sound," he replied, his voice deep with determination.

Her heart warmed and she reached out to grab his hand. She could walk through life's ups and downs with his big, warm hand wrapped around hers.

Still, she couldn't help but wonder how long this cozy safe haven Bo had provided her would last. Trey and his men had come up with nothing. She couldn't imagine who might be after her.

How long was she willing to put her life on hold, hiding away in Bo's house with fear as a constant, simmering companion? How long would Bo continue to live his life this way?

"You know I can't just stay at your house forever," she said.

"So far I'm not complaining," he replied easily. "I wonder if the ghost walker has anything to do with the new amusement park?" he asked, obviously changing the subject.

"No way. The ghost walker started making her appearance long before the amusement park bought the land to build. Besides, if it was somehow tied to the amusement park then it would be a ghost of a pirate in keeping with the theme," she replied.

"I thought all the ghosts of pirates past appeared at the Pirate's Inn," he said with a touch of amusement.

"That's the rumor. Supposedly old Peg Leg walks down the hallway on the second floor and you can hear his wooden leg as he walks. Then there's Pirate Joey, who is drunk on rum and stumbles around trying to find his ship."

Bo laughed. "Shelly worked as night manager there for years and never saw a ghost, although she used to tell me it was kind of creepy to work the night shift."

"Creepy how?"

"She occasionally heard noises like creaking and thumping. I told her it was probably nothing more than the building settling, but she still got freaked out occasionally."

They headed down the street that was one block over from Bo's house when she noticed the odd illumination that filled the night sky. "What's that?" she asked.

"Looks like something is on fire," Bo replied and squeezed her hand tighter as he pulled her into a fast jog. They reached Bo's street, where his house was in the middle of the block, and Claire gasped in horror.

The street was alive with activity. The town's two fire trucks were parked along the curb in front of Bo's house. A large group of nightwear-clad neighbors had clustered on the sidewalk across the street as flames shot out of Bo's house.

Two patrol cars were also parked on the street as she and Bo began to run toward the scene.

What had happened? Claire's mind raced. Had they left the stove on after dinner and had it somehow caught fire? Had there been an electrical weakness somewhere in the walls that had sparked into flames?

The volunteer firefighters, clad in their yellow jackets, trained hoses on the flames but they appeared to be making little progress at containment. Thankfully Bo's motorcycle was far enough down the driveway to not be in any immediate danger of catching fire or blowing up.

As they got close enough to feel the heat, Trey stopped them. "Thank God you two weren't in there," he said. "I was afraid we'd be looking for charred bodies in the morning."

"How did this happen?" Bo asked, his features grim in the unnatural dancing light of the fire and the cherry swirl of lights from on top of the various emergency vehicles and patrol cars.

"I can't answer that yet. Bob has been too busy working to talk to me," Trey replied.

Bob McDonnel was the fire chief and at the moment one of the men manning the hoses. "He'll be able to tell us more once they get a handle on the fire and he gets a spare minute. Right now they're trying to save your bike and make sure the flames don't jump to the houses on either side."

Claire felt Bo's frustration wafting from him as she stared at the burning house. As vicious and hungry as the flames appeared, she feared there would be nothing left when the fire went out. She was watching him lose his last tie to Lost Lagoon, the house where he'd grown up.

"By the way, where have you two been in the middle of the night?" Trey asked.

"We couldn't sleep so we decided to take a walk," Claire said. There was no reason for Trey to know they'd ventured out to see a ghost walk.

"Convenient that both of you just happened to be gone when the house went up in flames," Trey replied.

Bo stiffened. "Are you implying something?"

Trey hesitated a moment. "Not particularly, just looking at all the options. You have to admit that where you go, trouble seems to follow."

"Have you talked to Jimmy?" Bo asked.

"I haven't had time. I figured he was still at work at Jimmy's Place and not inside."

"I need to check in with him and make sure he

is still at work. I don't have my cell phone with me. Can I use yours?"

Again Trey hesitated, as if not wanting to do anything to help ease Bo's obvious worry. Finally he pulled his cell phone from his pocket and handed it to Bo. "Make it fast," he said grudgingly.

Bo took several steps away from Trey and Claire. "You don't think this is some kind of an accident, do you?" she asked Trey.

"Until I talk to Bob I won't know for sure, but my guess is that somebody was hoping to kill you or Bo or both with the fire."

Claire wrapped her arms around herself as icy chills walked up her spine. Thank God she hadn't been able to sleep. Thank God she'd decided to wake Bo and leave the house for a little ghost hunting. If they had been inside the odds were good that they both would have been overwhelmed by smoke and would have died for sure.

Bo walked back to where they stood and handed Trey his phone. "Thanks. Jimmy is fine and will stay in the apartment on the third floor at Jimmy's Place."

The fire had become less intense and Claire figured it would only be a matter of minutes before the firemen finally had it completely out. At least the frame of the house still stood, but that was small consolation as she thought of the damage within.

Bob appeared near the house and motioned to Trey and Bo. "I'll just stay here," Claire said. "There are plenty of people out and about. I'll be fine. Go talk to the fire chief and see what he has to tell you."

Bo looked around as if assessing the situation, and then with a curt nod he and Trey headed in the direction of Bob. Claire stared at the house, which would be smoke- and fire- and water-damaged. There was no question in her mind that it was a total loss.

At least they had her place to crash at. She would feel safe there as long as Bo was with her. Her chest tightened with emotion. Had this been a murder attempt or a tragic accident of some sort?

Had it been directed at Bo, or her, or both of them? A hysterical giggle rose to her lips and she swallowed it. The problem with hooking up with the man who was half the town's nemesis and gaining for herself some crazy nut stalking her was that when a hit came there was no way to predict exactly who it was directed at.

She suddenly realized that most of the crowd had dispersed, returning to their homes and their beds to sleep for what was left of the night.

A sharp sting struck the back of her shoulder. She swatted at it, accustomed to the gigantic mosquitos that ruled the evening and nighttime hours.

Within seconds she started feeling strange. Cotton began to wrap her brain, making it difficult for her to think. She started in the direction of Bo and the other men, but her legs grew wobbly. All of her muscles relaxed and her eyelids grew too heavy to keep open.

Someplace in the very back of her mind, she knew

she was in trouble. She tried again to take a step toward the house, but instead fell into darkness and knew no more.

Chapter Eleven

"It was definitely arson," a smoke-blackened face told Bo and Trey. Bob swiped at the sweat across his forehead with a soot-colored handkerchief. "The accelerant was gasoline. We found three gas cans on the back porch."

Bo felt as if he had fallen into somebody else's nightmare. He knew there was nothing salvageable about the house or its contents.

All traces of his childhood, anything left of his mother, was gone forever. He had insurance, but right now didn't think he had the heart to rebuild. He felt utterly defeated.

Somebody in this town had taken the life of his girlfriend, the town had spit in his face, and now the one thing he had left here was gone, burned by an unknown adversary.

Bob clapped him on the back. "Sorry we didn't get here sooner. If we'd gotten the call quicker we might have been able to save it."

Bo nodded. "I know you all did the best you can and I appreciate it."

"It's too hot to go in tonight, but I'll be here first thing in the morning to investigate thoroughly," Bob said.

"I'll be here, too," Trey said. He looked at Bo. "No matter what I believed happened two years ago I'm determined to find out who is behind this fire and the attacks on Claire. Personal feelings aside, I intend to do my job to the fullest of my ability."

"I appreciate that," Bo replied. The mention of Claire pulled his thoughts away from the house. He looked to the sidewalk across the street and realized it was empty of people.

Claire! His brain flashed with the beginning of panic. Where was she? He gazed over to where the firemen were loading up their equipment, hoping to see her talking to one of them. But she wasn't there, and the seed of his panic exploded into a full-blown alarm.

"I don't see Claire," he said aloud. He looked at Trey, as if the lawman could magically make her appear. "Claire is missing."

"She's got to be around here someplace," Trey replied. He called her name and Bo did the same, his heart beating a frantic rhythm that he heard in the sudden pounding of his head.

He ran across the street, still shouting her name, but there was no answering reply. He raced toward the fire trucks and asked each and every man he met if they'd seen Claire, but nobody had noticed her.

He ran back to where Trey stood in his front yard. Trey finished a call on his cell phone. "I've just called in every member of my team to check out the men who were on the list she gave me and to start a search for her. I'm going to check around back and make sure she didn't just wander around to see the damage and maybe got hurt."

"I'll come with you," Bo said, praying that there was an easy answer for Claire's absence and not the one that horrified him most.

He'd been distracted. He'd left her alone and now he feared that her stalker had taken advantage of the situation and had somehow gotten to her. If that was the case it was all his fault, and the thought of anything bad happening to her nearly brought him to his knees.

They reached the backyard, each of them calling her name. Desperation made Bo feel like everything was happening in slow motion. His backyard was not so big that he couldn't see in the glow of his flashlight that she wasn't there.

Somehow, someway, her stalker had taken her and nobody had any idea who that person might be. Bo's heart ripped in a hundred pieces as he could only imagine her fate at the hands of a monster.

"This is a first," Trey said from the back porch. "I've never seen an arson fire where the arsonist was so neat." He shone his flashlight on three gas cans, a small one, a medium and a larger, all neatly aligned side by side.

"Usually, a fire-starter empties the accelerant on the target, then tosses the empty can aside," Trey said.

Bo stared at the cans, his mind racing. Silverware

neatly aligned next to a plate…a chair placed in precise position under an umbrella table…and now three gas cans neatly arranged in a row.

"I know who it is," he said to Trey. "Claire's stalker is Roger Cantor. It's Roger Cantor," he repeated with urgency.

Trey frowned. "Coach Cantor?"

Wild panic filled Bo. "He set this fire and now he has Claire."

"How do you know?"

"I just do. Where does Roger live?" Every muscle in Bo's body tensed. Trey couldn't get the information to him fast enough. Every moment counted, every second might mean the difference between life and death.

"Over on Cypress Street. I don't know the exact address, but it's midblock between Pirate's Lane and Oak Street. He has a basketball goal in his driveway. Come on, I'll drive you there," Trey said.

The two men raced for his patrol car and once inside Bo fought an overwhelming sense of disaster. Had the fire been set as some sort of diversion? If so he had played right into Roger's hand. He'd taken his eyes off the prize and allowed Claire to be stolen away.

Trey couldn't drive fast enough to suit Bo, who kept his focus out the window checking for signs of somebody hiding or Roger carrying Claire away.

If Roger harmed a hair on her head, Bo would kill him. Trey would finally get his desire to see Bo locked up in prison. Bo didn't care. He had nothing to lose but Claire, and the thought of her gone forever was too much for him to bear.

Trey pulled into the driveway of Roger Cantor's house, a neat ranch that was dark. What if Roger was sound asleep inside and had nothing to do with Claire's disappearance? What if Bo had jumped to the wrong conclusion and they were just wasting precious time by coming here?

A million doubts coupled with a rage of adrenaline filled him as he and Trey approached the front door. Trey knocked as though he meant business, the rapping on the wooden door loud enough to wake the neighbors.

"Roger, open the door," he shouted.

Bo noticed Trey had his hand on the butt of his gun, obviously ready for anything they might face. What they faced was no reply. No lights went on and nobody came to the door.

Trey knocked again and Bo moved to the garage door, where small windows allowed him to see the dark shape of a car parked inside. "His car is here," he called back to Trey.

"He's not answering the door," Trey replied.

"Break it down," Bo exclaimed. His imagination filled with visions of Claire tied up and gagged in the basement or in a bedroom while Roger waited patiently for Trey and Bo to eventually go away.

"I don't have that authority," Trey replied. "I can't break into someplace based on your gut instinct alone. Let's check around back."

The two men raced around the side of the house,

where there was a patio and a sliding glass door, but no indication that anyone stirred inside.

Bo's heart beat so hard it felt as if it could explode out of his chest at any moment. He knew Roger was their man. His proof was in those neatly aligned gas cans.

He looked around and saw a large outdoor vase with flowers. He had to get inside and he understood Trey's being bound by the law, but he wasn't bound by anything except his driving need to find Claire.

He picked up the vase and threw it with all his might at the sliding glass door. The glass shattered and Trey cussed. Bo went in through the busted door, carefully avoiding the last of the shards of glass that clung to the frame.

Trey followed after him, muttering curses as he pulled his gun. They entered the neatest kitchen Bo had ever seen, a sign of the obsessive-compulsive disorder Claire had told him Roger suffered and that he'd seen signs of himself.

Trey motioned for Bo to stay behind him as they left the kitchen and entered the living room. They turned on no lights, using only their flashlights to illuminate their way.

Find Claire. Find Claire. It was a two-word mantra that echoed over and over again in Bo's head as they cleared each room in the house.

It was only when they entered the master bedroom that Bo's calculated guess that the stalker was Roger was definitely realized. Taped to the wall above the neatly made queen-size bed were dozens of photos of Claire.

Claire on her bicycle, Claire sitting on her front porch, there was even a photo of her taken through her bedroom window. Thankfully she'd been wearing a robe. They were slices of her life captured forever to feed a sick mind.

What frightened Bo most was that there were three photos of Claire and him together, eating ice cream, leaving Mama Baptiste's shop and getting into her car. In each of those pictures Claire's face had been x-ed out with a bright red marker.

"Here's your proof," Bo said to Trey. Bo whirled around and tightened his hand on his flashlight. "It's obvious they aren't here. Does Cantor own any other property in town?"

"I don't know. I'll have to check it out. I'll let all my officers know that we're looking for Cantor," Trey said.

There was no basement in the house, but there was an entire town to search. Bo's head screamed in pain and fear. "I'm heading out on my own," he said to Trey when they reached the front door.

Trey took his cell phone out of his pocket. "This is my personal phone. I've got another cell phone that is for official business. Take it so that if you find her you can call me, or if we find her we can get in touch with you."

"Thanks." Bo put the phone in his jean pocket and then with a grim nod to Trey, he took off into the night.

He ran in no particular direction, knowing only the driving need to seek and find, praying that it wasn't already too late. Roger could have her held captive in any old shed, in one of the abandoned shanties on the other side of town. Hell, he could have her stashed away in her own home.

With this thought in mind, he raced in the direction of Claire's place, slowing his pace only when he could scarcely breathe and was stabbed by a stitch in his side.

Claire…Claire… His heart cried out for her. A vision of her face filled his brain. Her beautiful eyes, that crazy mop of golden curls, the smile that made him feel wanted and loved, it all haunted him now.

He should have kept her tight by his side while the fire blazed at his house. He'd provided a perfect opportunity for Cantor to strike by being distracted, by allowing Claire to wander away from him.

My fault, he thought in agony. Just like Shelly's murder had been his fault. He should have gone to meet her that night despite being sick. If he'd just gotten out of bed and gone to the bench at the lagoon's edge, she wouldn't have been murdered.

If he'd just kept hold of Claire's hand, she wouldn't be gone now and in the hands of a man whose obsessive love had transformed into a killing hatred.

When he finally reached Claire's house he was shocked to see Eric Baptiste sitting on the front porch. "Nobody is here," he said to Bo.

"What are you doing here?"

"I ran into Deputy Griffin. He told me Claire was

missing and potentially kidnapped. Claire gave my mother a spare key to this place years ago. I got it and went inside and checked it out. There's no indication that anyone has been here and I'm sitting here all night to make sure nobody else tries to get inside."

It was the longest speech Bo had ever heard Eric make. "Have you checked out any of the abandoned shanties?"

"Not specifically, but I've been here awhile and haven't seen anything unusual. No lights or sounds coming from any of the old places."

Dead end. A new desperation crashed down on Bo. Where to go? Where would Roger go? Was it already too late? Had he already killed Claire? Desperation turned to horror as a new thought filled his head.

He turned and ran, not bothering to say goodbye to Eric. He couldn't speak with the emotion that clogged his throat. Was it possible? Was Roger sick enough to do such a thing?

The sound of his feet hitting against the road surface was the only noise he heard. He was so deep inside his head he heard nothing else, smelled nothing as he focused on getting to the place where Shelly's body had been found floating in the swamp.

Roger had to not only hate Claire, but Bo, as well. Would he have his revenge on both of them by making Bo face losing somebody he cared about and tossing her body in the same place where Shelly had been found?

PINE CLEANSER.

Claire tried to remember if she'd cleaned the shanty with pine cleanser that day. She usually bought the cleanser with money Mama Baptiste gave her. It was cheap and even though the plywood walls had gaps in them, despite the fact that her mattress was thin as paper and sometimes there was electricity and sometimes there wasn't, she liked to keep things clean when she could.

She couldn't remember the last time she'd seen her father. It had been at least two weeks since he'd shown his face at the shanty.

Mama Baptiste had tried to tell her that her daddy wasn't a bad man, he was a sick man. Alcohol had not only poisoned his body but had addled his brain, making him forget that he had a daughter, forget that somebody might need him.

Her bed felt particularly hard tonight...like concrete. She tried to shift her position and realized she couldn't move her legs. Brain-fogged, she thought she was trapped by the favorite blue blanket she always slept beneath.

She tried to reach a hand down to untangle herself, but her hands were bound together. That's when full consciousness slammed into her.

The fire at Bo's...the sharp sting in her back...and then nothing. She'd been drugged and now she was someplace she shouldn't be, a place that smelled of pine cleanser and a faint, lingering odor of sweaty socks, a place that screamed of danger.

She was afraid to open her eyes, scared of what

she'd see, of who might be in the alien space with her, even though she sensed that she was alone.

She finally worked up the courage to open her eyes. She couldn't begin to formulate a plan of escape unless she knew exactly where she was.

With her brain still slightly fuzzy, she took in the concrete floor beneath her and the concrete walls that surrounded her on three sides. It was only when she saw the round drains in the floor and the row of showerheads that she realized she was in the boys' shower room at the school.

Her ankles were tied together with a strong rope, as were her wrists. Just as she'd sensed, she was alone in the brightly lit room.

She managed to roll to a sitting position and then scooted across the floor until her back was against the farthest wall from the opening, an opening where sooner or later she knew she would meet her "admirer."

The severity of her situation sank fully in and tears sprang to her eyes. She was in trouble…life-threatening danger, and she worked her ankles and wrists, twisting and turning in an effort to get free of the ties that bound her.

However, there was no give to the rope and the knots held tight as a rising panic filled her. She had no idea how long she'd been unconscious and even if everyone in town was searching for her there was no reason for anyone to believe she was being held in a shower in a school that was closed for the summer.

She could scream, but she knew it would be no

help. The school building was surrounded by parking lots and playgrounds and she was in a concrete room. Nobody would hear her scream except the person who had brought her here.

She told herself to stay calm, but a terrifying panic rose up the back of her throat, making her feel nauseous. Under the circumstances she just couldn't help the terror that shuddered through her body.

"Hello, Claire." The familiar voice came from the darkened entrance to the shower.

"Hello, Roger," she replied, somehow unsurprised that it was him. Her brain had subconsciously made the connection when she'd realized she was in the shower room at the school. "What's going on?" She kept her voice calm as if this was all some sort of familiar game they played as they so often played basketball in the gym.

"You ruined everything, Claire. I had it all planned out in my head. It was all going to be so perfect and then you ruined it all and now you have to die."

Claire instantly realized she wasn't dealing with the man she'd played ball with, the man she'd shared so many lunches with both at school and in her home. Gone was the warmth in his eyes, replaced by a fire of simmering rage. His entire body was tensed and his hands balled into fists in a rhythmic pattern of one…two…three and then pause. One…two…three and then pause.

"What did I ruin, Roger?" She knew the only

hope she had of somebody finding them was to try to keep him talking as long as possible.

Time. At the moment time was her best friend. She needed as much of it as she could possibly get to give somebody an opportunity to find her.

"Everything," he screamed, his voice echoing in the shower chamber as the cords of his neck popped out.

Claire fought the terror that ripped through her at the raw hatred in his voice. Calm. She had to stay calm. "You said you had a plan. What was the plan, Roger?"

He swiped his hands down the sides of his face, took several steps into the shower and then leaned with his back against the opposite wall and stared at her. The rage in his eyes dissipated and was replaced with a soft look of dreams to come.

"I've loved you for a long time, Claire, but you know I had some issues I needed to work on. I worked hard to make my OCD manageable, and it was all because I wanted to be a good man for you. I finally got to the point where I felt comfortable starting my courtship."

"You were my secret admirer," she said. "You left the flowers on my porch. Why didn't you just come right out and tell me how you felt?"

"Because I had a plan. I needed to follow the plan," he replied impatiently, as if she were slow-minded. "The flowers and notes were just the beginning. I wanted you to believe your secret admirer was thoughtful and romantic."

"I did," she replied fervently. "I was charmed by the gifts left on my porch. I couldn't wait to meet the wonderful person who left them for me." It was a lie. Maybe she'd been charmed after the first couple of times, but the whole thing had become creepy and stalkerish.

"In my plan the next step was to invite you for pizza one night, just a casual meal that we'd share together."

"Like you'd planned to do with Mary," Claire said.

Roger snorted. "I was never interested in that insipid woman at the diner. She meant nothing to me. It was you. It was always you." He frowned. "I want you to hear the whole plan, so don't interrupt me again or I might lose my temper."

He began to pace, taking three steps in one direction and then three steps in the opposite direction. He didn't look at her when he spoke again.

"We'd have a casual pizza date and you'd start to see me not just as a coach, not just as a friend, but you'd feel a little romantic attraction toward me. After a week or so we'd have another date, this one at Jimmy's Place. We'd order the steak special and laugh and the chemistry would be amazing between us. At the end of that date we'd share our first kiss."

He paused a moment in his pacing and closed his eyes, as if imagining the kiss in his mind. Creepy-crawlies shot through Claire as every nerve inside her recoiled.

She realized she wasn't dealing with obsessive-compulsive disorder, but rather something deeper and darker. Roger was in a place in his head where she didn't want to go.

His eyes shot open once again and he stared at her. "The kiss would be magic and you'd know then that we belonged together. After that it would be you and me sharing ice cream at one of the umbrella tables or walking hand in hand down the sidewalks. On our third official date we'd have dinner at my place and that night we would make love."

He began to pace again. "After that it would be a whirlwind romance. Within two months we'd be engaged and in four months we'd be married and you'd never leave me. That was the plan, Claire. We were supposed to be together forever. Then you screwed it all up by hooking up with a bad boy on a motorcycle."

"Bo and I aren't hooked up," she said desperately. "We're just friends and I've been working with him to find out who killed Shelly Sinclair. He really means nothing to me."

"Liar!" Once again Roger's angry voice bounced off the walls. "I see the way you look at him. I see the way he looks at you. That's not friendship, it's lust and want and it wasn't supposed to be that way. You were supposed to be all mine."

"I didn't know the plan, Roger," she protested. "I didn't know that you were my secret admirer. It's not too late for us. We could have that pizza date and see how things play out."

"It is too late." He drew in a deep breath, his eyes

dead and empty of emotion. "You're tainted and now you need to be killed."

"Did you set the fire at Bo's to kill us both?" *Keep him talking*, she thought in desperation. Surely Bo was tearing up the town in an effort to find her. *Find me, Bo. Please find me*, her heart begged.

Roger nodded. "Do you know how many people die in their sleep from smoke inhalation? That was my first idea, but I had a backup plan. If the two of you managed to escape the fire, I figured there might be enough of a commotion around that I'd be able to grab you." He offered her a self-satisfied smile. "A smart man always has a backup plan."

"What did you give me to knock me out?"

"A little antianxiety medication. Trust me, over the years I've learned a lot about the doses and effects of those kinds of drugs. I should have drugged you that night at your mailbox."

"Why do I have to die?" Tears misted her vision and she consciously willed them away, not wanting him to see any weakness.

"Because I can't live my life and see you every day and be reminded of the plan that was supposed to make me happy for the rest of my life. You would just be a painful reminder of my failure and of your betrayal."

"Roger, you won't get away with this. You were already on a list of suspects after you attacked me at my house. They'll be looking for you and you don't have an alibi."

"I'll make one up," he said easily. "I'll tell them I

often have trouble sleeping and come here to shoot hoops. They won't be able to disprove it."

"If you kill me here, there will be evidence." Her desperation peaked as she realized she was running out of time.

"I don't intend to leave a blood trail. The only evidence they'll find is a damp towel and several loose basketballs in the gym, furthering my alibi."

"Then how do you intend to kill me?" she asked, knowing that despite the ropes she'd fight him in any way possible. Somehow, someway, she wasn't going to make it easy for him.

"I'm going to strangle you, Claire, and then I'm going to carry your limp, dead body to the lagoon and leave you where Shelly was left. I think the sheriff will find it a strange coincidence that Bo McBride came back to town and for a second time was intimately involved with a woman who is found floating in the lagoon."

A mind-numbing horror swept over her, not for herself, but for Bo, who would be forced to relive his traumatic past. He wasn't in love with her as he'd been with Shelly, but Claire knew he cared about her.

"I'm going to the gym now to set things up to substantiate my alibi. When I come back, then it's time…time to rid myself of you."

As he left the shower room the tears Claire had fought so hard to hold back released. She would never hug a little student again. She would never see Bo again, feel his arms wrapped around her, taste his hot, sensual lips.

The happily-ever-after she'd dreamed of with a special man ended here, in a pine-scented boys' shower room with a man who had gone to great lengths to end her dreams and end her life.

Chapter Twelve

Bo reached the lagoon and fell to his knees in relief when he found no body floating in the water. He didn't know how long he remained on the ground, emotions raging out of control and leaching physical strength from him.

The clock that had been ticking so loudly, so frantically in his head since the moment he'd discovered Claire gone had gone silent. His relief at not finding her here was short-lived, for he feared they were too late. She'd been gone too long.

He hadn't heard anything from Trey, letting him know that nobody else had been successful in locating Roger and Claire, and she'd been gone for well over two hours.

He couldn't stanch the emotion that erupted from the depths of him. Tears filled his eyes and raced down his cheeks, tears he couldn't stop as his heart felt her absence.

It wouldn't be long before the morning sun would peek over the horizon, making the search a little easier, but also bringing with it a sense of hopelessness he didn't want to face.

He wanted her found before the sun came up. He needed to hold her in his arms before a new day broke. Where could they be? Apparently Trey had found no record of any other property Roger owned, otherwise he would have called Bo.

He finally managed to pull himself to his feet and walked over to the stone bench and sank down. His brain was in utter chaos, making it impossible for him to think clearly as he swiped away the tears.

Had Roger borrowed or stolen a car? Was it possible the two of them were no longer even in the town of Lost Lagoon? If that was the case then they could be anywhere within a two-hour drive.

Think, Bo demanded of himself. If he were Roger Cantor where would he take Claire? Roger Cantor, seemingly nice guy, battling OCD and beloved coach at the school. Nerves jumped inside him.

The school! Bo knew Roger had a key to the gym door. It would be a familiar place, somewhere he would feel safe. Bo jumped up from the bench, his heart beating so fast he was half dizzy.

He took off running, hoping he was right and that it wasn't already too late. The school was on the opposite side of town, but Bo had no intention of pacing himself.

He ran all out, as if he were a high school athlete trying to make the track team. He ignored cramping calf muscles and the stitch in his side, focused only on getting to the place where Claire might be with her monster.

Although he knew deputies were out searching, he didn't see anyone as he raced to the only place that suddenly made sense. It had to be the school, and if they weren't there, then he was lost and defeated.

Would he be in time or would he find Claire injured or, even more heartbreaking, dead? He couldn't think about that now, for if he did he'd lose it, and he needed to keep it together now more than ever before.

He hadn't been able to save Shelly. He needed to save Claire and that need drove him forward faster than he'd ever run in his entire life.

When the school came into view, it appeared to be a dark, uninhabited fortress. No lights glowed at any of the windows. He finally slowed his pace to catch his breath as he moved from the front of the building to the back.

There were no cars in the parking lot, but Bo knew that Roger was physically fit enough to carry Claire anywhere he wanted her to be.

By the time Bo reached the back door that led into the short hallway and the gym area, his breathing had returned to normal despite the race of his heart and a new adrenaline spike.

He reached out for the door handle and caught his breath as the door clicked open. They were here! He stepped into the dark hallway and looked just ahead where the gymnasium was dark, as well.

Then he heard her scream. Every nerve in his body jumped in response as he tried to discern where the scream had come from. He took several steps forward and peered into the boys' locker room. The main area, where the students had their lockers and changed clothes was dark, but a light shone in the shower area.

Bo surged forward at the same time he heard Claire scream again. He entered the shower to see Claire on the floor and Roger on top of her, apparently trying to strangle her.

Bo roared with rage as he threw himself forward. At the same time Roger turned and rolled to his feet to meet Bo's attack.

She's alive, the words screamed in the back of Bo's head. But he knew she wouldn't be for long if he didn't manage to somehow neutralize Roger.

The two men met in the center of the shower and began throwing punches at each other like a couple of bar brawlers. Bo was taller but Roger was stockier. Roger was driven by self-preservation, but Bo was driven by the need to protect Claire at any cost.

Roger landed a punch to Bo's stomach that momentarily took Bo's breath away, but he recovered by slamming an uppercut into Roger's chin. Roger stepped back and shook his head, but then charged Bo once again, this time using his leg in an effort to sweep Bo's feet out from beneath him.

Bo managed to stay on his feet but Roger slammed him with a fist to the eye. The only sound in the shower was the slap and punch of hits and the grunts and heavy breathing of the two men as they battled.

Bo realized the two of them were evenly matched

when it came to throwing punches, and that was when he remembered the knife he'd tucked into his pocket earlier in the evening.

He managed to gain enough distance from Roger to pull out the knife and open it. But the moment he held it out before him Roger surprised him with a perfectly delivered kick that sent the knife out of his hand and sliding across the concrete floor.

Both men lunged for the weapon. Roger reached it first and threw his body over Bo's. Bo grabbed the hand that held the knife pointed at his heart.

"No!" Claire screamed, making the first sound she'd made since Bo had appeared.

Bo's entire body trembled as he fought to keep the knife from plunging into his body. "You should have stayed away from Lost Lagoon." Roger's breath was hot and fetid on Bo's face. "You should have stayed away from her."

"Roger, your plan was stupid and would have never worked because I secretly thought you were nothing but a creep," Claire said fervently. "I would have never dated you or belonged to you in any way. You're nothing to me, Roger, and no matter what your plan you would have never been anything to me."

Her words had power, for Roger weakened and in a flash Bo managed to grab the knife and roll on top of the man. Bo held the knife to Roger's throat.

Bo had never entertained a homicidal thought in his life until that moment. He wanted to kill Roger. He wanted the man dead for touching Claire in any way, for terrorizing her and trying to take her away forever from Bo.

His hand at Roger's throat shook slightly. Roger's eyes were huge as he stared up at Bo, waiting for death to be delivered.

"Bo." Claire's voice cut through the killing rage that threatened to consume him. "You aren't a killer," she said softly. "Don't become what some people still believe you are."

Bo's hand shook harder as he fought an internal battle, the need to destroy the man who'd sought to destroy Claire and the desire to stay true to the man he believed himself to be.

He finally tossed the knife aside and delivered a punch to Roger's face that rolled Roger's eyes up in the back of his head and rendered him unconscious.

Bo instantly got up, grabbed the knife once again and hurried to where Claire was huddled in the corner. Neither of them spoke as he cut through the rope around her ankles and then through the binds around her wrists.

It was only when she was free that he pulled her up off the floor and into his arms. He held her tightly, as if afraid that somebody might try to rip her away from him again.

She began to cry, her face burrowed against his chest as tremors raced through her. He caressed a hand up and down her back, murmuring soft assurances that she was safe and nobody would ever hurt her again.

At the same time he kept an eye on the unmoving

Roger. He had no idea how long the man might stay unconscious and he didn't want to go another round with the athletic coach.

Claire's tears finally ebbed and he released her. "I need to call Trey, but first I want to make sure that Roger doesn't come to and have more fight left in him."

He picked up the ropes he'd cut off Claire and used them to tie Roger's wrists together. The man still appeared to be completely out.

Once that was done, he grabbed the phone Trey had given to him to use and by searching the contacts found the number to call to reach Trey on his official business cell phone.

With the phone call made, Bo led Claire out of the shower enclosure and into the main locker room, where he turned on the lights and then pulled her to sit next to him on one of the wooden benches between the walls of lockers.

"I didn't think anyone would ever find me," she said, her voice still holding a tremor that spoke of the terror she'd suffered.

"Thank God I figured it was Roger before I left the scene of my house." He explained to her the careful alignment of the gas cans that had been the clue he'd needed.

"Trey and I checked his house first. One wall of his bedroom was filled with pictures of you. He's apparently been stalking you for a long time."

Claire shivered and he wrapped an arm around her shoulders and pulled her closer against him. "When we didn't find you at Roger's place, Trey and I split up," he continued.

He told her about going to her home and finding Eric there, then his mad dash to the lagoon, afraid that history would repeat itself.

"That's what he intended to do with my body," she said. "He was going to strangle me and then take me to the lagoon and leave me floating in the water where Shelly had been found. Thank God you thought about the school."

She shook her head. "I was stupid. I allowed myself to be vulnerable."

"I was the stupid one. I let the fire distract me and left you vulnerable. But it's over now, Claire. You don't have to be afraid anymore."

She looked up at him, her blue eyes filling with tears once again. "But you lost your house because of me."

"No, I lost my house because of Roger," he countered. "Besides, I have insurance and it will all get sorted out."

Trey and several of his men came into the locker room. "Claire, I'm glad to see you're okay," he said and looked around. "Where's Roger?"

"In the shower," Bo replied.

"Did you kill him?"

Bo stood to face the nemesis who had done everything in his power two years ago to see Bo behind bars for the murder of Shelly. "I had a knife at his neck. I had every opportunity, every reason in the world to kill him, but I didn't because that's not who

I am. It's never been who I am. I wasn't a murderer two years ago and I'm still not a killer."

Trey motioned his men to the shower enclosure and then he pulled a notepad and pen from his pocket. "I need to get initial statements from both of you."

Bo gazed at Claire's face. Exhaustion played on her pale features. He looked back at Trey. "Very brief statements," he said. "We can come into the station sometime later this afternoon for complete statements, but right now it's almost dawn and everyone is exhausted."

True to his word, Trey kept his questions brief and few and then re-pocketed the notepad and pen. "We can finish things up later."

Bo gave Trey back his cell phone and then together he and Claire walked out of the school, leaving Trey and his men to deal with Roger and sort out the crime scene.

A faint glow of pinks and oranges lit up the eastern sky as they walked toward Claire's house. Morning birds began their songs as the weight of exhaustion fell on Bo's shoulders.

"You know you're welcome to crash at my place for as long as you need to," Claire said.

"I'll take you up on that offer at least until I figure things out. Right now I'm so tired I can't think."

She grabbed his hand. "I'm glad to be so exhausted. It means I'm still alive. I stared madness in the eyes tonight and I'll never be able to thank you enough for riding to my rescue."

He squeezed her hand. "I just couldn't imagine what would happen if I lost my boss," he said with forced lightness.

"After tonight you get to be the boss all the time," she replied.

He laughed. "I have a feeling after a couple of hours of sleep you'll feel differently about that."

"You're probably right," she agreed.

By that time they had reached Claire's house, where Eric still sat on the front porch. He stood. "You're okay?" he asked Claire.

"I'm okay," she replied.

Eric nodded, handed her the spare key to her house and started to walk down the sidewalk toward Mama Baptiste's place. Claire called after him and he turned to face them. "Thank you," she said.

"No problem," he replied and then turned and continued to walk away.

Claire opened the door and Bo followed her inside, closing and relocking the door behind him. "Do you want anything?" she asked. Her features were drawn and a deep exhaustion showed through the dull shine of her eyes.

"Sleep," he replied. "We both need some sleep."

"There's no reason for you to sleep on the sofa. You can sleep with me in the bedroom."

He knew it was no invitation for anything but rest and perhaps the need of a woman who had been to hell and back and simply wanted the comfort of somebody sleeping next to her, hopefully keeping nightmares at bay.

In the bedroom she pulled the blinds closed and then collapsed on the mattress. He did the same and cuddled her in his arms. She snuggled against him, a perfect fit against his body.

She released a weary sigh and was asleep almost immediately. With the sweet scent of her hair and the smell of her perfume permeating the room, Bo also fell into a deep, dreamless sleep.

CLAIRE WOKE FIRST, with Bo spooned around her backside. She didn't move, not wanting to break the utter peace she felt with his body so close against hers and one of his arms thrown over her.

He had been like an animal protecting his mate last night in the shower stall. He'd fought for her with a ferocity that had awed her.

Love for him swelled up inside her, chasing away any bad memories that might attempt to intrude. She loved his strength of character, his courage in agreeing to remain in town and face the people who had condemned him as a murderer.

She loved his dry sense of humor, the way his lips slowly slid upward into a smile that almost felt like a precious gift. She'd thought herself to be falling in love with Bo, but realized now there was no falling… she was deeply in love with the man. He was everything she wanted for her happily-ever-after and yet she knew deep in her heart it wasn't meant to be.

He had given her no indication that he felt the same way about her. Sure, he'd saved her life, but he'd promised to be her bodyguard.

Partners with fringe benefits, that's the way he thought of them, not lifelong lovers sharing a future together.

She wasn't even sure if he'd stay in town beyond tomorrow. The call to return to his life in Jackson would be stronger now. His home here was gone, the danger to her had been vanquished, and she had a feeling the will to clear his name had been more her idea than his.

A glance at her clock let her know it was just after noon. She should get up but she was reluctant to stir, afraid that she'd awaken Bo. Besides, these moments being held in his arms would someday be precious memories she'd carry with her for the rest of her life. She closed her eyes once again and just existed in the warmth and security of Bo.

"Are you awake?" His warm breath caressed the back of her neck.

"Wide awake," she replied and opened her eyes. He pulled his arm from around her and she sat up. "I've just been thinking about having to go into the station today and relive what happened last night." It was a little white lie, but she couldn't very well tell him she'd been thinking about how much she loved him.

He sat up and swung his legs over the side of the bed at the same time he raked a hand through his hair. "I'll be right beside you and hopefully it won't be too rough on you. At least you lived to tell the tale."

"Thanks to you," she replied.

"Besides going into the station, I've got a ton of things to take care of today, the first being buying some clothes and then getting in touch with my insurance company and figuring out what comes next."

She wanted to ask him what did come next. Was he staying or going? She almost hoped he decided to go back to Jackson. She'd be left with a heart broken in two, but there would be no more opportunity for her love for him to grow even deeper.

"Let's get the interviews with Trey over with first," he said. "Then I can bring you back here and I'll take care of some of my own business."

"Sounds like a plan," she agreed and stood. "I'm going to shower and change clothes and then you can shower. Unfortunately I don't have anything that will fit you for you to change into."

He grinned, that sexy smile that only managed to begin the breaking of her heart. "I'd worry a little if you did have clothes that fit me. I'm fairly open, but I draw the line at hanging out with a cross-dresser."

Claire threw a bed pillow in his direction and then walked to her closet to grab clothes for the day. Bo left the bedroom and headed for the kitchen, where Claire figured he'd have a pot of coffee ready by the time she'd showered.

Minutes later she stood beneath a steamy spray of water and tried not to think about Bo McBride. Instead she forced herself to go back to the night before and the time she'd spent with Roger.

She would have never guessed him to be a stalker...her stalker. They'd shared a great relationship as coworkers and friends, but she'd never dreamed he had become obsessed with her.

Had she missed telling cues? Had she not noticed something that she should have realized was off between them? She'd never felt any odd vibes coming from him.

It didn't matter now. He would be going away for a long time and the danger to her was finally over.

The scent of freshly brewed coffee greeted her as she stepped out of the bathroom. Bo was seated at her table with a cup in front of him.

"The bathroom is all yours," she said and poured herself a cup of coffee.

"I called Trey and told him we'd be in within a half an hour or so. It's a good thing you still have a landline because both our cell phones are probably melted into ash mounds."

"I kept the landline because cell phone reception is a bit spotty in the house," she replied. She sat at the table as he stood.

"It won't take me long and then we can head out and get the interviews over with." He disappeared into the bathroom.

Claire sipped her coffee and tried not to think about Bo naked in her shower. Drat the man anyway and damn her for allowing him to get so deeply into her heart. She certainly hadn't been looking for love when she'd ignored George and thrown a burger and fries to Bo.

True to his word, he showered and re-dressed in a matter of minutes and then they were on their way to talk to Trey. Claire had thought that emotionally she'd handled the ordeal just fine, but when she had to relive the details of the horrendous night she broke down.

It was only Bo's presence, his hand on hers, that allowed her to get through it all. She then listened to Bo give his statement and finally they were finished.

They swung by Bo's house and she was surprised that the outer shell still stood. The windows had been blown or broken out, the paint was dark with soot, but the good news was that his motorcycle, parked in the driveway, appeared to be undamaged.

"Thank God the garage was full of boxes that I was going to give to charity, otherwise I would have parked inside and the bike would be gone," he said.

"What about a key?" she asked.

He turned off the car and smiled at her. "I've got a spare in a combination lockbox I had welded to the inside of the saddlebag just in case of an emergency." He pulled the keys out of the car ignition and handed them to her. "At least I have wheels to take care of some business. Why don't I plan on being back at your house between six and seven?"

"Okay," she agreed. "I've got a few errands I need to run, too, so I'll see you at the house later."

She got out of the car and got into the driver's seat he'd vacated. Only when he had his spare key in the ignition of his motorcycle and she heard the throaty roar of the engine did she drive away.

Her first order of business was to get a new cell phone. She also needed to stop by the bank and get a new credit and debit card. She'd also have to go to the motor vehicle bureau and get a copy of her driver's license.

Her brain spun as she tried to think of everything that had been in her purse…a purse now burned to a crisp in the fire. If she was lucky she could accomplish everything, stop by the grocery store and pick up a few things, then have a good dinner waiting for Bo's return to the house.

It was five o'clock when she finally got home and unloaded the groceries she'd bought. She'd managed to get everything she needed to do done and had planned a meal of a salad, spaghetti with meat sauce and garlic bread for dinner.

She got the meat sauce cooking and made the salad, and it was only as she set the table for two that she realized how difficult it was going to be for her if Bo stayed here for an indeterminate period of time.

Two plates on the table looked right. Her house was a perfect size for her, but would be an intimate setting with Bo sharing it.

He hadn't mentioned a word about leaving town and she could only assume he intended them to pick up where they'd left off before danger had reached out to her. Could she go back to investigating Shelly's death with him at her side, with him staying in her house?

She suddenly felt vulnerable and far too fragile. She'd never even felt this way when she'd been alone as a child and the darkness of night had been a very scary place.

Bo returned at six thirty, carrying a new duffel bag with new clothes and toiletries and with an energy that filled the house, making it immediately shrink to minuscule size.

"Hmm, something smells good," he said. He walked across the room and tossed his duffel bag into the bedroom.

"And your timing is perfect," she replied with a forced lightness. "It's ready to be served."

"Great. I'm starving. Is there anything I can do?"

"No thanks, I've got it."

He sat at the table and while they ate he told her about what he'd accomplished during the afternoon. She shared her afternoon activities with him and while she did she was struck by the domestic scene created.

They were like husband and wife, coming together over a meal to share the events of their day. The domesticity continued when they'd finished eating and Bo helped her clear the table and clean the kitchen.

This was the happily-ever-after she'd dreamed about when she'd been young. The filling in of a loneliness she'd suffered for most of her life, the sharing of both simple and complicated things. But this couldn't be her happily-ever-after. Even though Bo was the right man, she was the wrong woman in the wrong place.

By the time they sat on the sofa Claire's nerves were completely shot. She turned on the television and stared blankly at the screen. Bo sat next to her, close enough that she could smell the scent of a new sexy cologne, feel the heat of his body radiating toward her.

He would just assume that tonight he'd share her bed and why wouldn't he assume that? She'd opened her home to him, opened herself to him in a way she hadn't intended and now knew she couldn't continue with her emotions in such turmoil.

"Are you okay?" he asked gently after several minutes of silence had passed.

She turned to look at him and to her horror she burst into tears. He instantly reached for her, but she scooted back from him and held up her hands to keep him away.

If he held her right now she wouldn't do what she knew had to be done. If he touched her in any way she wouldn't be strong enough.

"I'm sorry, Bo," she managed to say through her tears. "I thought I could do this… I thought I could have you here with me and it would be no big deal. We'd continue on like we were, investigating and spending all our time together. But it is a big deal because…because I'm totally in love with you." She held her breath and watched the stunned expression sweep over his handsome features.

"That wasn't supposed to happen," he finally replied.

She brushed the tears from her cheeks and drew a deep breath. "I didn't exactly plan it. All I know is I can't do this. I can't spend my days and nights with you as if I'm not in love with you. I can't play at being partners in crime when I want to be partners in life forever."

He frowned and scanned the room, as if lost and trying to get his bearings. He finally gazed at her, a wealth of sadness in his eyes. "I'm sorry, Claire. I don't know what to say."

What he hadn't said, said it all. He hadn't proclaimed his love for her. He certainly didn't appear happy at her pronouncement of her feelings for him.

"There's nothing to say," she replied. "I can't change the way I feel, and I certainly can't make you feel something you don't. You were straight with me from the very beginning. I just didn't realize that I wasn't in control of my own emotions."

He stood from the sofa and walked to the bedroom, where he grabbed his duffel bag and then headed for the front door. She watched him covetously, her heart already beginning to splinter.

"I owe you so much, Claire," he said and opened the front door. "I just want you to know that I've appreciated your help and your belief in me."

"You saved my life last night. I figure we're even." She fought back a fresh wave of tears. "Are you planning on sticking around town or heading back to Jackson?" she asked.

"I think it's time I put Lost Lagoon behind me," he replied. "Goodbye, Claire."

He disappeared out the door and it was only when she heard the roar of his motorcycle that her heart completely shattered and she allowed the tears to overwhelm her.

Chapter Thirteen

Bo headed toward Jimmy's Place, knowing that there was plenty of room in the upstairs apartment for him to bunk there until he decided what he was going to do.

Stay or go?

Claire's confession of love for him had shocked him. He hadn't seen it coming, although perhaps he should have. Driving down Main Street he thought of the softness of her gaze when she looked at him and the passion she'd shown him when they'd made love.

The way her hand had so often sought his, how easily she'd smiled at him, he should have realized she was into him, but he'd been completely blind to the depth of her emotions where he was concerned.

The knowledge of her love weighed heavy on his heart. He'd never wanted her to love him. Love had no place in his life. He was a man marked as a murderer, a man who had decided never to allow himself to love again.

Stay or go?

He parked his bike behind Jimmy's Place. Just

inside the back door in the kitchen area was a set of stairs that led up to the apartment on the third floor.

The apartment door was unlocked, as he'd expected it to be, and as he stepped inside the wide-open space of combined living room and kitchen, memories from a different life slammed into him. There were three doors; two led to bedrooms and one to a bath.

This was where he'd lived when his father had been alive and Bo's Place had been a roaring success. He and Shelly had stolen private time here until his father had passed and he'd made the decision to move back with his mother, who he felt needed him at the time.

He opened the door to the smallest bedroom, knowing that Jimmy had taken up residency in the master bedroom. He tossed his duffel bag on the bed and then headed back downstairs.

He needed a drink. Hell, he needed a hundred drinks to erase the vision of Claire's tearstained face from his head. She was in love with him. He'd broken her heart, so why did his heart ache so badly?

He slid onto the stool he'd sat in the last time he'd been here. Jimmy was behind the bar and ambled toward him. "Glad to see you aren't a crispy critter, and I was happy to hear that Claire is okay," Jimmy said and opened a bottle of beer and placed it in front of him.

"Unfortunately the house is a total loss," Bo said. "I'm sorry about your things."

"It was just things," Jimmy replied easily. "I just

can't believe that Coach Cantor was such a nutcase. By the way, where is Claire now? You two have been like Mutt and Jeff since you came back to town."

Pain shot through his heart and he took a sip of his beer before replying. "She told me she's in love with me." Bo hadn't meant to lay it out like that, but the words just slipped from his mouth.

Jimmy didn't look surprised. "I figured you two had a mutual thing going on. It looked to me like you were as much into her as she was into you."

Bo looked at his friend in surprise. "I was into her. She's sexy and smart, amazingly centered, what's not to like?" Bo paused to take a sip of his beer, the icy liquid tasting bitter. "But you know I have no intention of inviting anyone into my life again on a romantic basis."

"Your mother would be disappointed to hear you say that," Jimmy replied. "Her greatest hope for you was that you'd get married, have a family and find real happiness despite what happened to you here. She hoped your bitterness would eventually disappear."

"I'm not bitter," Bo replied wearily. It was true. The bitterness he'd arrived in town with was gone, and he knew much of the reason had been Claire.

"So, how did you leave things with Claire?" Jimmy asked.

"We said goodbye, you have a roommate for the night and tomorrow morning I'm heading back to Jackson." Just that simply he made up his mind. It was time to leave.

"What about sticking around and finding out who killed Shelly?"

A dry laugh released from Bo. "It was a stupid idea. It's been too long, and without any law enforcement backing there's no point in trying to solve a crime."

"And the killer just gets away?"

Bo shrugged. "He's gotten away for the last two years. For all I know the person who killed Shelly isn't even in town anymore. I need to get back to my life in Jackson and put all this behind me forever."

He took another drink of his beer in an effort to banish the vision of Claire that continued to fill his head.

"What are you going to do about your mother's place?" Jimmy asked. "You know I'm good staying upstairs. I was only there for your mother."

"I know, and I appreciate it. To be honest, I don't know what I'm going to do about the house yet," Bo replied. "Probably rebuild and then sell."

"You know I'll be glad to be your point man if that's what you decide to do. You hire the contractor and I'll see that he and his workers stay in line."

Bo smiled at Jimmy. "I don't know what I would have done without you over the last couple of years."

"And I don't know how I would have survived my childhood and be where I am now without you," Jimmy countered. "Will you still be around when I get up tomorrow?"

"I doubt it. I'm planning on taking off around nine, but you know we'll be in touch often." With Bo still the official owner of Jimmy's Place and now the matter of his mother's burned home, he and Jimmy would always have reasons to remain in close contact.

Bo finished his beer and waved off the offer of another. Exhaustion weighed heavily on his shoulders, or perhaps it was the memory of Claire's tears that made him feel like a broken, soulless man.

When he got back upstairs he got into bed and stared at the dark ceiling, wishing he could stanch the visions of Claire that danced in his head.

She'd be fine without him, he told himself. She was a survivor. She had a job she loved and people who loved her here. Eventually she'd forget all about him. He'd become just a bad memory like her childhood.

She was too bright, too beautiful to be alone for long. She was optimistic by nature and deserved a man far better than him. She'd find that man and live the happily-ever-after she'd dreamed about.

The thought brought him small solace as he finally fell asleep.

HE AWAKENED JUST after seven and showered and dressed. Jimmy's bedroom door was closed and Bo had no intention of bothering his friend before he took off.

He made a pot of coffee to fuel up for the long ride back to Jackson and then poured himself a cup and sat at the table. He tried to keep his thoughts schooled to the future and not dwell on what would soon be the past.

Still, he had to admit to himself that, despite the danger, it had felt good to be back in Lost Lagoon. This was and always would be home to him, no matter where he decided to live out the rest of his life.

By nine o'clock, juiced up on caffeine, he slung his duffel bag over his shoulder and left the apartment. He stowed the bag and then climbed on the motorcycle and headed down Main Street.

Everything had gone down so fast, so unexpectedly, with Claire the night before. He hadn't really gotten the chance to thank her for being his friend, for wanting to be his partner, and more important, for believing in him.

Her unwavering belief in his innocence had healed some wounds, had given him back his dignity and made him realize it didn't matter what people in Lost Lagoon thought about him; he knew what kind of man he was, and that was enough for him to move forward.

He'd had no intention to see Claire again, but found himself parked outside her house. Just a quick goodbye, he thought as he climbed off the bike.

She opened the door before he knocked, apparently hearing the arrival of his motorcycle. She allowed him inside and then backed away from him. "I figured you'd be halfway to Jackson by now," she said.

"I'm getting a late start and I didn't want to leave town without telling you once again how much I've appreciated your support." His words sounded stiff and he felt tongue-tied.

Maybe this would have been easier if she didn't have on the turquoise T-shirt that so perfectly matched her beautiful eyes. Maybe goodbye would have been easier if she didn't look so beautiful with the morning sunshine glinting in her hair and a look of soft vulnerability on her features.

He laughed suddenly as he realized he hadn't stopped for a final goodbye. He hadn't wanted one last conversation with her before he left town.

Her eyes widened at his laughter and she took a step backward, as if he might be losing his mind. "Bo, what are you doing here?"

He took several steps toward her, his heart beating faster. "I thought I came by here for a final goodbye, but now that I'm here looking at you, I realize I came by to tell you I love you."

She stared at him in disbelief and he took another step toward her, knowing that what he said next would the most important words he would ever say to a woman, that this was a chance at true happiness that so far had been elusive to him.

"I don't want to go back to Jackson. Despite all the odds against me here, Lost Lagoon is where my heart is…and I believe it's because you are here."

She didn't appear happy; rather, she looked confused. "But what about your life, your business in Jackson? How would you live, how would you survive, here in Lost Lagoon?"

"I can break my lease on my rental home and

stay here with you until we rebuild the house. My manager at Bo's Place in Jackson has hinted more than once that he would be interested in buying the business from me if I ever decided to sell." He took another step toward her, pleased that this time she didn't back away.

"As far as making a living here, I still own Jimmy's Place." Her eyes opened wider and he continued, "Nobody in town knows that I didn't sell out to Jimmy. Money isn't an issue if I stay here, but there's only one reason I would decide to stay and you gave that to me last night when you told me you loved me."

"You didn't exactly appear happy when I told you how I felt about you," she replied, her eyes still holding wariness, but also a faint shine of hope.

Bo walked forward until he stood so close to her he could lean forward and take her lips with his. "You shocked and awed me last night when you told me you were in love with me. I'll admit, my first instinct was to run. I'd sworn to myself that I'd never allow anyone deep in my heart again, but somehow, someway, you got in so deep I can't imagine living my life without you. I love you, Claire, and I'd be all kinds of fool not to stay and see if there's a happily-ever-after for us."

The wariness was gone from her eyes and instead he was bathed in the love that poured from her. "Are you going to kiss me now?" she asked impatiently.

He laughed and pulled her into his arms and kissed her with all the love, all the passion that burned in his soul for her. They might not have been able to clear his name yet, but the love that filled his heart was more than enough for him to know true happiness.

"Does this mean I get to be boss again?" she asked once the kiss had ended.

He laughed again. "I think that issue will continue to be one that's negotiated on a regular basis. Right now I'm boss and I'm going to kiss you again."

"Fine with me." She barely got the words out of her mouth before his lips took hers again.

Bo knew it wouldn't be easy to stay and face the people who still believed he was responsible for Shelly's death. But never had Lost Lagoon felt more like home than at this moment, with Claire in his arms.

This was where he belonged, and this was the woman who owned his heart. Hopefully Shelly's murderer would eventually be found, but in the meantime he had a happily-ever-after to give not only to a woman who had earned it, but to a woman who held his own forever happiness in her hands.

* * * * *

Don't miss the next romance in
Carla's exciting series,
coming fall of 2015
from Harlequin Intrigue!

COMING NEXT MONTH FROM

 HARLEQUIN

INTRIGUE

Available May 19, 2015

#1569 TO HONOR AND TO PROTECT
The Specialists: Heroes Next Door
by Debra Webb & Regan Black
Addison Collins will do anything to protect her son. But can she protect her heart from former Army special forces operative Andrew Bryant, the man who left her at the altar—and the only one she can trust to safeguard their son?

#1570 NAVY SEAL NEWLYWED
Covert Cowboys, Inc. • by Elle James
Posing as newlyweds, Navy SEAL "Rip" Cord Schafer and Covert Cowboy operative Tracie Kosart work together to catch the traitors supplying guns to terrorists. But when Tracie's cover is blown, can Rip save his "wife"?

#1571 CORNERED
Corcoran Team: Bulletproof Bachelors
by HelenKay Dimon
Former Navy pilot Cameron Roth has no plans to settle down. When drug runners set their sights on Julia White, it is up to Cam to get them both out alive...

#1572 THE GUARDIAN
The Ranger Brigade • by Cindi Myers
Veteran Abby Stewart has no memory of Rangers lieutenant Michael Dance, who saved her life in Afghanistan. But when she stumbles into his investigation, can he save her from the smugglers stalking them?

#1573 UNTRACEABLE
Omega Sector • by Janie Crouch
After a brutal attack leaves her traumatized, a powerful crime boss forces Omega Sector agent Juliet Branson undercover again. Now, Evan Karcz must neutralize the terrorist threat and use his cover as Juliet's husband to rehabilitate her.

#1574 SECURITY BREACH
Bayou Bonne Chance • by Mallory Kane
Undercover Homeland Security agent Tristan DuChaud faked his death to protect his pregnant wife, Sandy, from terrorists. But when her life is threatened, Tristan is forced to tell her the truth—or risk both their deaths becoming reality...

YOU CAN FIND MORE INFORMATION ON UPCOMING HARLEQUIN® TITLES, FREE EXCERPTS AND MORE AT WWW.HARLEQUIN.COM.

HICNM0515

REQUEST YOUR FREE BOOKS!
2 FREE NOVELS PLUS 2 FREE GIFTS!

H HARLEQUIN®

INTRIGUE

BREATHTAKING ROMANTIC SUSPENSE

YES! Please send me 2 FREE Harlequin® Intrigue novels and my 2 FREE gifts (gifts are worth about $10). After receiving them, if I don't wish to receive any more books, I can return the shipping statement marked "cancel." If I don't cancel, I will receive 6 brand-new novels every month and be billed just $4.74 per book in the U.S. or $5.49 per book in Canada. That's a savings of at least 12% off the cover price! It's quite a bargain! Shipping and handling is just 50¢ per book in the U.S. and 75¢ per book in Canada.* I understand that accepting the 2 free books and gifts places me under no obligation to buy anything. I can always return a shipment and cancel at any time. Even if I never buy another book, the two free books and gifts are mine to keep forever.

182/382 HDN GH3D

Name	(PLEASE PRINT)

Address	Apt. #

City	State/Prov.	Zip/Postal Code

Signature (if under 18, a parent or guardian must sign)

Mail to the **Reader Service:**
IN U.S.A.: P.O. Box 1867, Buffalo, NY 14240-1867
IN CANADA: P.O. Box 609, Fort Erie, Ontario L2A 5X3
**Are you a subscriber to Harlequin® Intrigue books
and want to receive the larger-print edition?
Call 1-800-873-8635 or visit www.ReaderService.com.**

* Terms and prices subject to change without notice. Prices do not include applicable taxes. Sales tax applicable in N.Y. Canadian residents will be charged applicable taxes. Offer not valid in Quebec. This offer is limited to one order per household. Not valid for current subscribers to Harlequin Intrigue books. All orders subject to credit approval. Credit or debit balances in a customer's account(s) may be offset by any other outstanding balance owed by or to the customer. Please allow 4 to 6 weeks for delivery. Offer available while quantities last.

Your Privacy—The Reader Service is committed to protecting your privacy. Our Privacy Policy is available online at www.ReaderService.com or upon request from the Reader Service.

We make a portion of our mailing list available to reputable third parties that offer products we believe may interest you. If you prefer that we not exchange your name with third parties, or if you wish to clarify or modify your communication preferences, please visit us at www.ReaderService.com/consumerschoice or write to us at Reader Service Preference Service, P.O. Box 9062, Buffalo, NY 14240-9062. Include your complete name and address.

HI15

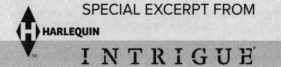
"How do I know you really work for Hank?"

"You don't. But has anyone else shown up and told
you he's your contact?" She raised her eyebrows, the
saucy expression doing funny things to his insides. "So,
do you trust me, or not?"

His lips curled upward on the ends. "I'll go with not."

"Oh, come on, sweetheart." She batted her pretty green
eyes and gave him a sexy smile. "What's not to trust?"

His gaze scraped over her form. "I expected a cowboy,
not a…"

"Cow*girl*?" Her smile sank and she slipped into the
driver's seat. Her lips firmed into a straight line. "Are you
coming or not? If you're dead set on a cowboy, I'll contact Hank and tell him to send a male replacement. But
then he'd have to come up with another plan."

"I'm interested in how you and Hank plan to help.
Frankly, I'd rather my SEAL team had my six."

"Yeah, but you're deceased. Using your SEAL team

would only alert your assassin that you aren't as dead as the navy claims you are. How long do you think you'll last once that bit of news leaks out?"

His lips pressed together. "I'd survive."

"By going undercover? Then you still won't have the backing of your team, and we're back to the original plan." She grinned. "Me."

Rip sighed. "Fine. I want to head back to Honduras and trace the weapons back to where they're coming from. What's Hank's plan?"

"For me to work with you." She pulled a large envelope from between her seat and the console and handed it across to him. "Everything we need is in that packet."

Rip riffled through the contents of the packet, glancing at a passport with his picture on it as well as a name he'd never seen. "Chuck Gideon?"

"Better get used to it."

"Speaking of names…we've already kissed and you haven't told me who you are." Rip glanced her way briefly. "Is it a secret? Do you have a shady past or are you related to someone important?"

"For this mission, I'm related to someone important." She twisted her lips and sent a crooked grin his way. "You. For the purpose of this operation, you can call me Phyllis. Phyllis Gideon. I'll be your wife."

Don't miss
NAVY SEAL NEWLYWED
available June 2015 wherever
Harlequin Intrigue® books and ebooks are sold.

www.Harlequin.com

HARLEQUIN®
A *Romance* FOR EVERY MOOD™

Love the Harlequin book
you just read?

Your opinion matters.

Review this book on your favorite
book site, review site, blog or your own
social media properties and share
your opinion with other readers!

Be sure to connect with us at:
Harlequin.com/Newsletters
Facebook.com/HarlequinBooks
Twitter.com/HarlequinBooks

HARLEQUIN®

A *Romance* FOR EVERY MOOD™

JUST CAN'T GET ENOUGH?

Join our social communities
and talk to us online.

You will have access to the latest
news on upcoming titles and special
promotions, but most importantly,
you can talk to other fans about your
favorite Harlequin reads.

Harlequin.com/Community

Facebook.com/HarlequinBooks

Twitter.com/HarlequinBooks

Pinterest.com/HarlequinBooks

HSOCIAL

HARLEQUIN®

A *Romance* FOR EVERY MOOD™

Stay up-to-date on all your romance-reading news with the *Harlequin Shopping Guide,* featuring bestselling authors, exciting new miniseries, books to watch and more!

The newest issue will be delivered right to you with our compliments! There are 4 each year.

Signing up is easy.

EMAIL

ShoppingGuide@Harlequin.ca

WRITE TO US

HARLEQUIN BOOKS
Attention: Customer Service Department
P.O. Box 9057, Buffalo, NY 14269-9057

OR PHONE

1-800-873-8635 in the United States
1-888-343-9777 in Canada

Please allow 4-6 weeks for delivery of the first issue by mail.